COMMUNITY SECRETS AND LIES

A DI Huws Crime Thriller-book 2 of 3

ANNE ROBERTS

Words Without Walls

To my sister and parents who have to laboriously read through my offerings before editing.

To my friend Wendy Challis-Jones who sowed the seeds of this story.

Chapter One

DI IDRIS HUWS slithered ungraciously down the steep slope, a mixture of gravel and moss moving in unison under his thoroughly unsuitable footwear. More Columbo than bear Grylls. He wasn't dressed for hillwalking or climbing this morning, or to be brutally honest, for most other work mornings if it came to it, but what will be will be. He tried to look composed, as if he had fully intended to slide down towards the small gathering of uniformed officers down below, like a windmill impersonating ballet dancer. He was convinced a couple had sniggered as his arms flailed to achieve some modicum of balance and dignity.

It was a while since he had been down to this area of the island, two years in fact since the so-called murders, that turned out not to be murders. He had spent a lot of time and effort on that case only to be thwarted by a wild animal at the end of it all.

His late wife Gwen had always nagged him to get himself a little fitter as it would improve his overall balance and agility when she dragged him out into the hills. It still very much felt wrong to say to himself, his late wife, it broke him up for a few minutes just to think about her. She was still very much his first waking thought, every day crushing him when the reality hit. It caught in his throat what-

1

ever he was doing or wherever he was at the time. She popped up in his mind always when he least expected it and it still stopped him in his tracks.

Gwen had died suddenly and unexpectedly last year, a massive heart attack had been the cause, according to his good friend Emyr Rowlands the local pathologist. She would have known nothing about it, she died in her sleep.

He himself however had been devastated by the suddenness of it all. Shocked to the core, she was always the one out walking for miles and nagging about the crap he ate at work. At least he had stopped his vaping, his effort to cut out cigarettes, Gwen always claimed they were a new unknown and no doubt like cigarettes, would be found to be lethal in years to come. Her death had thrown him totally off kilter for a time, but once everything had been organized and sorted regarding the burial and family concerns, work had helped. He knew full well however it was just delaying the full wrath of grief.

This year since March 2020 had been the strangest time of his life to date - a global pandemic, Covid-19 had changed the whole world, created friction in all quarters, set people against each other, the anti- covid, anti- vaxxers, in fact the sort of people who appear to be anti-everything, against the rest of the population who were scared to death of contracting this disease or giving it to their families.

His working life had become one of constant bloody mask wearing, hand washing and sanitizing until the skin on his hands became dry as a crisped autumn leaf.

His life had changed further after Gwen's death when his widowed mother had invited herself to live with them, to care for him and his by now 17-year-old daughter. Not his choice, but he hadn't been in the right place within his head to resist or create a reasonable excuse. It was difficult being treated like a ten-year-old again. Part of him was pleased that she had come, as it would have made checking up on his old mum difficult through the lockdowns. She also conveniently enjoyed walking the family dog.

It was now nine months, and nothing seemed to be getting any better, but for the police and the other emergency services, life seemed to just go on the same. Still having on occasions to deal with the dross of life with no allowance for Covid or anything else for that matter.

The two officers below him were stood just at the edge of the ledge, masked and gloved as per the new guidelines, nothing to do with the fact that ten feet below them wedged in a crack in the rock-face, was the body of an as yet unknown person. Partly submerged, his hair floated in fronds around his head like a mat of fine seaweed. They hadn't been able to climb down to him or reach down towards him without risk of a slip, so a call had gone out to the local lifeboat station, the call initiating an immediate launch by the always-ready crew. They would be there shortly.

"What information do we have if any? Who found the body?"

Huws looked from the officers towards a young lad who stood to his right, "Y fi", he answered, "Sorry, me" he repeated. "I live just up the road and come here often to fish". Huws knew that he mentioned that he lived locally as part of a habit, a way of pre-empting accusations of Lockdown rule breaking.

"I was on that headland, across just there", as he pointed to the left, "The fishing is better off there than here, your gear doesn't tend to get snagged on the rocks at mid tide, I had just cast and was just looking around for any feeding birds when I saw it. I thought it was just a piece of clothing but came across to check anyway. I leant over and had a look; it is face down and I'm not even sure if it is a man or a woman". The poor lad sounded in part upset but also as if this was the most exciting thing to ever happen to him.

"Was there anyone else in the area during this time, that might have seen anything?" asked Huws.

"He already asked me that," replied the lad nodding towards the officer nearest him. "There were a couple of people who had walked off Fedw fawr over there, but they got straight in their car and drove off up the lane, that was before I noticed that". Another nod of the head towards the unfortunate body. "I hope the lifeboat is here pretty soon, they haven't much time before the tide is at its highest and it will likely be submerged then".

Literally as he finished the sentence, they turned their heads as the thrum of the twin engines of the Lifeboat came into view in front of Ynys Seiriol, its front raised high out of the water to then sink gracefully down as the engines slowed, leaving an ever-widening wake behind them. They hung back, away from the headland awaiting instructions. Thankfully despite the summer drawing to its end, there was no wind to carry away the shouts of the constable as he pointed down below him.

The orange clad crew appeared to chat amongst themselves as one clambered onto the bow looking down into the clear depths, obviously looking out for any underwater hazards as he gesticulated with his free hand for the helmsman to proceed with care. They were soon alongside the unfortunate person who was now gently bobbing face down in the gentle lift and fall of the wake as it reached the shore.

Whilst the people present concentrated on the goings on offshore, three fluorescent coated people scrambled in a slightly more dignified and practiced manner down the slope than Huws himself had done no more than ten minutes ago.

"Hi, I'm Aled, Station officer with the local Coastguard team, we have been paged to maybe assist in stretchering a casualty up to the car park?"

"Ah right, however, we just need to wait on the scenes of crime officers before I can authorize removal, if you can just maybe hang around close by for a while, maybe have someone ready to help the SOCO team carry down any equipment that they might need."

"Sure," responded Aled, before speaking into his hand-held radio, obviously communicating with the rest of his crew up in the car park.

"You do know that we were here as a team last night don't you, to the injured but totally piss...uhm, inebriated fisherman, he quickly corrected himself. He had slipped and fallen and had a lower leg injury and a badly cut face, though, once we had struggled to carry him up the slope to the top, his leg injury appeared to not bother him too much anymore, and suddenly less drunk, he refused to go in the ambulance and promised us he was just going to walk home, though I notice that the car that was there last night is not there now."

This was certainly news to Huws, "Who rang for help then?"

"He did that himself apparently," responded Aled. "He refused to give us either a name or address, more than likely because he was breaking lockdown travel rules. We've had that happening all summer with this Covid situation. People all over the beaches who we know are definitely not locals, because they, fair play to them, stay indoors or walk locally. It's been a huge problem for us, but we've no powers to police it. Early on in the summer, we did do mutual patrols alongside your people, to advise beachgoers of social distancing and stuff, but we generally just got sworn at."

"So basically, we have no idea who it was? Could it be possible that it is the body in the water, would you recognize him?" asked Huws.

Why was nothing straight forwards when he was in this area. He slightly regretted that he had chosen to be an active DI, boots on the ground, as opposed to being office based. That would bore him totally.

"Are you willing to have a look and see if we can link him to last night's incident?"

"Of course," responded Aled. "Dyfed my deputy was on the call as well, between the two of us I'm sure we can either eliminate or identify him as the same person."

Huws asked the officer to direct the lifeboat crew to turn the body over if it was possible.

They got as close as they could, one of the crew members reaching across towards the rock face to stabilize the boat and prevent the slight swell from pushing it onto the rough rock surface. Another stepping across with one leg, placing it firmly on a small ledge, his other leg firmly on the inflatables rigid side. In this position, he bent down and struggled to slightly lift the body by its clothing and turn it face up. The clothing that was snagged onto a spike of rock lifted loose.

The ghoulish white face, eyes open, already taking on the distinct swelling of water absorption, that can hide normal features, looked up at everyone, unseeing and unable to tell his tale. Huws looked towards Aled and Dyfed who were peering over the edge alongside the young fisherman who Huws seemed to have forgotten was there.

"Oh my God" he exclaimed; he looks horrible." Huws directed an officer to take the young lad away, his part in the proceedings done for now.

Aled and Dyfed were looking and chatting amongst themselves before Aled gave a definite shake of his head and said, "No, that is definitely a different man."

"Are you sure?" asked Huws, "It may be difficult because he has been in the water a few hours or more."

"No definitely not the same man, different features, different hair colour and style, and this person has a beard, last night's man needed a shave but hadn't got a beard. He had a distinct cut on his right cheek, I should know because I cleaned it and dressed it for him while waiting for the ambulance crew."

His colleague Dyfed who had been called down by radio had agreed.

Down the steep slope behind them scrambled a couple of coast-guard volunteers bedecked with bags, followed by a couple of white overalled, wellington'd forensics officers.

The decision was thankfully made quite quickly that the body could be bagged and taken by boat to the town slip where an under-taker would be notified to await the return of the crew. The crew struggled slightly as it became clear that the body was also snagged by his belt not just his coat, just below the surface, hence tethering him securely to the rocks, he was heavy and his clothes waterlogged, but eventually came free. He was carefully placed in a body bag with difficulty on the small floor area between the inflatable edge and the seats, sadly they seemed well practiced and adept at this task.

Idris Huws felt a sense of déjà vu as he remembered the last time, he had been in this situation just two years ago in a bay just west of where they were now. The difference this time though was that he chose to don a lifejacket and travel back with the body rather than make a fool of himself scrambling back up the slope to the car park. He instructed one of the officers to drive his car back to the town and pick him up when forensics had secured the scene. The second unfortunate officer was destined to be stuck here now until they had completed their investigations, though by the lack of any obvious evidence at the scene they wouldn't take too long. The clue to solving this was finding out who the mysterious casualty was from last night's Coastguard call out. A further chat with the Coastguard team members later was needed to see if they could shine a light on anything useful. They were making their way to the lifeboat station too.

Chapter Two

ARRIVAL AND DEPARTURE from the lifeboat station were as dignified as these things could be, Huws clambered down off the back of the boat, struggling to remove himself from the constraints of his lifejacket with cold, wind-stiffened fingers, before handing it to a crew member. He stepped across to where Aled the Coastguard station officer was waiting for him, trying to pat down his breeze blown hair.

Before Huws could open his mouth Ceri a female Coastguard officer handed him a black bin bag. He took it, waiting for a reason.

"This is what I picked up last night around where the man we treated was, rather than leave all his rubbish down there. It is mainly a couple of beer cans, a baseball hat, empty chip shop packaging, a box of matches and a small blanket, the type with a waterproof side that people use for picnics. There was no fishing gear down there though which is surprising considering he said he had been fishing, I used gloves so I wouldn't put my fingerprints on them."

Pleased with herself for appearing knowledgeable in crime procedures, knowing full well she only had gloves on because they had to.

"Thank you," said Huws, not opening the bag. He supposed they may be able to use some of it to gain evidence some prints if nothing else.

"Do you think there is a connection between the two men then?" asked Aled. "Dyfed here says the car was a maroon-coloured Skoda Octavia estate, he would notice these things, he's a mechanic. He even remembered the first part of the reg number as he didn't pay that much attention to it, EL42 he said. I don't know if that's of any use."

Huws nodded in acknowledgement, "No idea on the man's name or where he was from, did he have a particular accent?"

"Well, I probably talked to him more than the others did as I dealt with his cuts, but he appeared initially intoxicated and slurring, I would say though with a fair degree of confidence that he had a southern accent, as in southern England not Wales. I asked him a few times what his name was, but I won't repeat his answers, let's just say he was less than cooperative. As soon as the ambulance arrived, I was pleased to hand him over. As far as I understand from the crew, he refused treatment, said he was fine and that he was going to walk home. They let him, there isn't much we could do, he wasn't violent, we didn't think it warranted calling you out, and he set off up the lane walking. He miraculously seemed to have sobered up, so I think he may have been putting that on a bit. We packed up and followed the ambulance up the lane, but we didn't pass him en route so it is fairly plausible that he doubled back or hid inside a gateway until the coast was clear and then could collect his car and drive to wherever he was staying."

"You don't think he was local?" asked Huws.

"Well, I can't be sure, but as a team we're pretty well spread around the area and none of us that were there early hours recognized him, mind you most of our casualties are usually from away anyway," added Aled.

Huws thanked them for their input and thanked Ceri for her useful rubbish collection duties. She gave him a cheeky thumbs up and returned both hands into the pockets of her overlarge overalls.

Huws returned to his car and made to leave for the hospital mortuary when the young officer who had bought the car there for him stepped across and asked whether he could have a lift back to station as his vehicle was still in the clifftop car park until the other officer was released from the scene.

"You can come with me to the hospital," he said, "Then I'll drive you back when I go on to the station."

"Do you mean to the post mortem?" asked the young man a tad nervously.

"Yes, have you been present at one before?"

"No Sir, I haven't," he answered.

"You will be fine, it's not the same as the old days when you were in the same space as the corpse with ten fags in your mouth and half a pot of Vicks stuffed up your nostrils making your eyes run as if you were crying like a baby. It's more clinical now, we will be in a separate room with a speaker and there will be a screen to watch, so you can pretend to be watching Silent Witness on TV," said Huws with a chuckle. The young officer seemed cheered slightly by this and visibly relaxed.

"I've never driven a car this old either" he added to fill the silence. "Is it an antique? you know, a classic car?"

Huws grinned, "Well, I suppose it is by now. It's a Ford Granada, belonged to my father, it goes well, simple to maintain, not like these computerized engines they have now. A bit heavy on the juice mind you. MOT exempt now which is good as it does sometimes smoke a bit."

"I've never driven an automatic before, it's quite a cool car. It feels huge, all that bonnet in front of you."

Huws smiled to himself again, knowing this was just nervous verbal diaorrhea on the part of the young constable. Filling the gaps in order to keep his mind off what was ahead of him. Huws had been in this same position himself. He understood and humoured the young man with random car chatter.

They pulled in to the small car park closest to the mortuary, cigarette butts blown into the pavement corners, discarded by past visitors. They entered the double doors into the poorly lit outer corridor which seemed appropriate considering the building's function. On then to another doorway where Huws pushed the communication button to draw the attention of whoever may be inside today. He was pleased moments later to see the welcoming smiling face of Jane, the pathology assistant whom he had met on most of his previous cases. He knew she was smiling only because of the twinkle in her eyes, the rest of her face was hidden behind a mask and visor. He hated all this but was guaranteed by the powers that be that it was the only way to go.

"I wondered if it might be yourself that came this time, Idris. Emyr thought it might well be, good to see you again." She walked ahead of them towards Emyr Rowlands the senior pathologist's office.

"Yes, good to see you again too Jane, but it would have been better to have met in happier circumstances than here." She gave him a quizzical look but turned into the next room. He was quite surprised that she had remembered his first name from a fair time ago now. It quite pleased him, though he had no idea why that might be.

Emyr Rowlands stood up, putting his hand out in greeting which was immediately pulled back. "Bloody Covid," he muttered as he remembered. "I refuse to do that silly Boris elbow tap," he added. They chatted for a few minutes about the situation of the world in general, chatted about how Huws was managing without Gwen, and the changes to his own work in the world of post mortems due to all the Covid regulations, how he was actually doing far less post mortems particularly if the word Covid was bandied about in any shape or form. No post mortems were needed if the person had supposedly tested for covid, regardless of any other medical reasons they may have had- equally likely to have killed them.

During this time Jane had returned to the autopsy room where she had, as per procedure, been photographing the man fully clothed before undressing him and preparing him for Rowlands to take over. Any ID that would have been on the man at the time would have been removed at the scene, bagged and handed in to the police SOCO team. Huws hadn't as yet spoken to the team, preferring to just get this part over with, for now at least.

He sat with his young companion in the observation room, Rowlands had his back to them, but this was not an issue with the camera directing its gaze at the body before him and transferring the image directly onto the screen on the observation room wall. They could well have been standing right next to the pathologist.

"I would age him at around fifty or so by first look," started Rowlands, "he's in fat to obese body condition, and I suspect that he has been in a bit of a fight, bruising to the upper arms and cheeks."

"Could that have happened falling into the water?" asked Huws via his microphone.

"Well, it is known that bruising can happen post mortem, in this case from a fall, but in fact if someone is handled roughly even up to nearly two hours after death, you may get some bruising, which can often indicate that someone was in fact moved after they died."

"Ah right," responded Huws. "So, he may have just fallen down the rocks and drowned?"

"Or someone killed him then threw him in." Piped up the young constable, seemingly quite engrossed and very interested in the proceedings down below.

"Let's not get ahead of ourselves," said Huws.

"Well, he does have a point, both things are totally plausible," nodded Rowlands, at which point the young officer smiled, pleased with himself.

"What's your name lad?" asked Huws, recognizing his rude failure in not asking his name.

"PC 1002 Parry," he said. "Steffan Parry."

"Right then Parry, you seem to be enjoying yourself, if this had been like it was for my first post mortem, I doubt you would be looking as bright eyed and bushy tailed as you are now, but well done for your enthusiasm. We will wait and see now what else Mr. Rowlands discovers."

The next part of the proceedings was the part that Huws liked the least, the removal of the top of the skull, not the sight but the sound of the small bone saw that was used.

Rowlands looked up at them both and stated that the brain showed signs of a bleed towards the base of the skull, a serious head injury which may well be the cause of death. From here on the autopsy continued as per normal until Rowlands then declared that the person on the table had not drowned but had obviously been dead when he entered the water, there was no evidence of froth in his upper airways or his trachea or any water in his stomach, there was a significant amount of alcohol and a chip supper in his stomach though. This put a slightly different view on it. Rowlands further declared that his heart had looked as healthy as he would expect, well at least for a man in the casualty's body condition, some tiny evidence of ischaemia on its surface but likely not as yet something which would have caused him significant angina. It more than likely ruled out that he had suffered a cardiac episode before a fall. Rowlands concluded that at this stage without the evidence of toxicology, the man had fallen or been pushed, suffered a significant head injury before falling over the edge into the sea, but considering the Coastguard call out the night before that they had discussed, it was also highly probable by the bruise marks on his upper arms that he had been manhandled over the edge. "Now it's your job to find out the tale that our body cannot tell us."

He left Jane to finish the minutiae of recording all the findings before yet another victim of a possible crime was slid back into its chilly home for the foreseeable future, the same special fridges that the two other victims had been in during the investigation of his previous cases in the locality. This method of refrigeration would allow the bodies if needed, to be stored at a colder negative temperature allowing for further investigation to be carried out without decomposition. Huws shared this information with PC Parry, as if he was party to this information first hand and not just educated in these facts by Rowlands previously. Parry seemed suitably impressed. Huws drove back to the station, Parry, yattering on all the way about the likely reason the man had been in the water. Huws certainly had to credit him with a very fertile imagination and a more severe case of verbal diaorrhea than he had initially imagined. Concluding in his head that he had been just as keen at one time in his career, he himself now however, suffered severe disillusionment and a lack of faith in human nature. He wondered how long it would take for young Parry to become the same.

Hopefully there would be a bit more information waiting for him when he got back to the office, he certainly hoped they had made some in-roads into finding the guy who had been at the scene last night and no doubt could fill in a few gaps.

Chapter Three

A FEW MILES along the coastline there was a flurry of excitement and a thudding of feet running down the lane that led to the lifeboat station. The first lot to get there would crew the boat that sat shining and ready for duty atop its steel railed tracks down to the sea. The doors would already be opening, the shore crew chomping at the bit to release the boat from its tethers, taut and pulling like an impatient horse ready for a sprint start out of the stalls. The all- weather Tamar class lifeboat would be needed for today's job. The first six or seven that turned up would be getting changed into their teddy bear fleeces and their all-in-one dry suit and boots, carefully zipping each other up to prevent ingress of water. A personal flotation device slung on and finally a white helmet with the weather protecting visor. All aboard, the lifeboat would slide down to meet the water creating a mini tidal wave with a wake strong enough to overturn any unfortunate kayaker nearby who had been foolish enough not to heed the warning of the launch.

The crew settled to their posts and positions, the Coxswain already studying the course plotted on the spaceship-like displays before him.

There was a degree of adrenaline involved regardless of the level of experience, they could never be a hundred percent sure as to what they would find at their destination. The Island based Coastguard Operations room had received a Channel 16 mayday call from a tanker moored out in the huge expanse of Red Wharf Bay. They were nine miles out at anchor, waiting for the boat from Amlwch to drop off a Pilot to see them into the Mersey docks when the tide was right for them. There were only four crew on board, such was the ease of sailing these great ships nowadays and one of those was the ship's cook. It was he who had seen the grey inflatable on their starboard side close into the ship, tucked in near her bow. He thought it strange that it hadn't shown on the ships radar, however he knew that it was likely at the moment that the rest of the crew were feet up watching the telly. His biggest cause for consternation however was the sight of two people, he believed to be two men, who were collapsed in the boat, one almost between the two powerful engines, the other slumped across the motorbike like helmsman's position. Neither had responded to his shouts, not that they would likely understand Polish, but the significant amount of blood that was swilling around the bottom of the boat dispersing into the sea behind them with each wave, probably made a response unlikely.

He walked up the metal steps, never one to panic, and in his mind a waste of energy considering the state of the men below. Sure enough, the crew were watching TV but soon got up when he told them they had visitors but that they were likely dead.

They made their way down below and opened a port access door almost at sea level. By now the boat was bobbing along towards the stern, bumped along with each little breaking wave, and likely to bob on by if they didn't try to do something to secure it.

Using a grapple hook on a length of rope they managed to catch onto the emergency buoyance aid holding bar across the back of the boat and pulled it closer. The captain was already making his emergency call to the Coastguard, giving them their position on the chart. "Zostrali zasrtrzeli," shouted the nearest, this message was passed to the captain on the bridge via his hand-held VHF radio. They heard the captain's response.

"Both male. Dead. Looks like they've been shot, over."

Chapter Four

HUWS STEPPED INTO HIS OFFICE, having left Parry to go his own way, no doubt to fill his colleagues in on the details of the autopsy. As soon as he put his bottom down in the tired old desk chair, a face appeared around the door.

"DI Sir, we have the lifeboat bringing in a dinghy with what we are told are two dead men on board, they were instructed to tow the boat around to the pier in Menai Bridge which is the easiest place for the team to get there."

This would be the same team that were no doubt now finishing off at the location of that morning's body.

"Christ this is like that saying where no bus comes for ages then three come together. I'll meet SOCO down there, it's only a few hours since I left. Can you ask DS Howard to meet me there too?"

DS Howard had been working with him on the previous murders, but in the two years that had lapsed, he had achieved a promotion that is not oft heard of in the police, he had been promoted straight from Constable to Detective Sergeant. Intelligent, enthusiastic and easy to get on with, but more importantly as far as Huws was concerned, plenty of common sense and no inflated ego. Feet firmly on the floor.

"In fact, can you find PC Parry too? I'm sure he would like to be involved."

With no chance to even grab himself a coffee, Huws grabbed his coat and made for his car, clearly it was going to be a long day.

It was still warm as he stepped outside. He had warmed up eventually after his chilly, wind-blown lifeboat ride, the long afternoon becoming a barbeque demanding evening. He speed dialed his own house, still unused to hearing his own mother answer the phone instead of Gwen, it gave him a kick in the guts when it happened.

"Hi mam, will you just put my dinner on a plate for me, I have no idea what time I'll be home, another job has come in. Talk soon." He knew he had been short and not given her a chance to speak, but unlike his Gwen who never asked for details unless it was offered, his old mum was a devil for gossip, so he reckoned if she didn't know she couldn't tell.

It only took twenty minutes to get to the pier. Parry was there, keen as mustard, ahead of him standing at the ready at the shore end of the pontoon which was currently sloping steeply downwards as the tide was at its lowest.

"Stay here for the time being please Parry, just to keep any nosey parkers from coming down onto the pontoon."

"Right, you are Sir," a distinct note of disappointment in his answer. Huws pulled his mask out of his pocket and put it on, along with a fresh pair of gloves, cursing under his breath again at its identity stealing discomfort. He saw the crew were tying up alongside the pontoon, the grey dinghy behind it, a bright orange survival bag covering what were obviously the two bodies. Huws hated the slight seasick inducing feeling he got when he ever set foot on these floating pontoons. He introduced himself to the crew member who had tied up the boat.

"Has anyone touched anything other than put the covers on?"

"Uhm, no Sir, in fact we only put the orange cover on as we approached Beaumaris and came down the Strait, we didn't want anyone to see the men."

"Good thinking. The team will be here in a bit, once I have had a chat with them, they will more than likely clear you to go, thank you for turning out." "It's our job Sir," responded the crew member.

Chapter Five

HE SAT ON THE BED, coat on and a woolly hat. It was bloody freezing in the cottage, despite it being still technically summer, and quite sunny outside. Thick walls, and small windows no doubt keeping the late summer warmth out. At least the electric supply was still on and the small heater broke the chill a tad. If he stayed mainly in the bedroom with the door closed it trapped the heat in with the curtains shut. The bedroom was at the back of the cottage, unseen from the track unless you were actually in the back garden.

He knew the owners lived miles away in England and due to the travel restrictions, they would not be allowed to visit. He knew this because of the visitor's book in the house. Telephone numbers for emergencies, Sussex number according to Google. Why anyone would turn the heating off completely in an old stone cottage like this was unbelievable, just the age of the house indicated that the walls would be running with damp come spring. Well, it wasn't really his problem and it certainly wouldn't be in a few days or so when he left, he just needed to keep his head down until he guessed the coast was clear for his getaway.

The car was out of sight of prying eyes of which there seemed to be hundreds, lockdown having created a new generation of walkers. Every hour of the day, every day, individuals and whole families walked past talking and laughing, anyone would imagine it was a national long holiday and not a bloody pandemic, hence the closed curtains. No one would know he was there.

Breaking in had been a doddle under the cover of darkness, a quick reccy for any evidence of CCTV cameras, no immediate neighbours to hear the shattering of the second bedroom window pane. He had let himself in and then opened the door to let Ricky in with his load of shopping bags. He would at least have plenty of food and drink to keep him going for a week or so, particularly now that Ricky was no longer part of the plan. Not his plan anyway. Ricky had been part of their plan, but not his. His plan had worked better than he had imagined. He wouldn't say it was easy, but it had been quick, and if it hadn't been for him hurting his leg, no one else at all would have known anything about it. The ambulance crew were quite satisfied to let him make his own way and from there and it had been a simple matter of popping through a nearby kissing gate and hiding around the corner till they and the Coastguard vehicle had driven off. Throwing the pistol into the undergrowth beyond the gate, he then walked back to the car. He couldn't help himself but whistle a jaunty tune to himself into the darkness, wondering how things may pan out come daybreak, but he was happy.

Cool as a cucumber he had thrown a portion of his rewards into the compartment under the boot floor and taken himself back to the cottage. He slept the deep sleep of a satisfied man that night.

Chapter Six

THE MEN LAY naked side by side on their individual tables. Rowlands was walking around them like a cat on the prowl, likely, wondering where to start. Idris Huws once again sat up in the viewing room, PC Parry standing up next to him, notebook open and a slightly less enthusiastic DS Howard sitting nearer the back. Huws cursed the steamed-up blindness that the mask he wore created on his spectacles, a sign of his age he supposed, he decided he could see enough without his glasses.

"Both Caucasian males," started Rowlands, "I would guess at an initial estimation before tests that they are both in the 30-40 age group. Well-built and fit looking. Both have gunshot wounds, and again a pretty accurate assessment before I start a detailed autopsy, both shot at close range. This one nearest to you a no doubt fatal shot to the head, the bullet entering his crown and exiting at the forehead."

"Shot from behind then?" asked Huws.

"Well yes, if we are stating the obvious," answered Rowlands with a glance in their direction. "The second man here may well have initially survived his gunshot wound to his abdomen but succumbed to blood loss in I would estimate a fairly short time.

Does that add up to your view of the situation?" Rowlands looked up towards them.

"God knows yet," responded Huws. "We have no idea of their situation and how they came to be around nine miles off the coast, is it possible that one could have shot the other before shooting himself?"

"Well yes, that is certainly one possibility, but until we look at the ballistics forensics aspects we won't know for sure, but, you know I haven't come across many people who have shot themselves in the back of the head, or in the abdomen, so if you want my professional opinion , then no, I don't agree with that theory. More than likely, both were shot by a third party possibly whilst they were leaving the scene. Was there a gun in the boat?"

DS Howard looked at his notebook and answered in the negative, no gun had been found in the boat, but since the design of the dinghy meant the stern was low into the water at the back between the engines then it likely could have gone overboard, along with two bodies worth of blood."

The remainder of the autopsies were concluded, DS Howard had twitched and shuffled throughout the proceedings, Parry had been hanging off every word uttered by both Rowlands and Huws, no doubt his overactive imagination making up some dramatic story to fit the situation. The results of the more intricate tests would be sent to Huws as and when they were available.

The other concerns around the occurrence were partly in the hands of the Coastguard ops room. They were looking into the mapping system to see if any tracking was available as regards the boats journey, unfortunately at this stage as the RIB did not have any form of safety tracking features on board that was not an easy task. The tankers that were anchored in the vicinity at the time were being contacted one by one just in case anything had been seen of the dinghy earlier in the day, either actual sightings or radar indications. No one seemed to have seen or noticed it so far being that it may well have entered the area under cover of darkness. It was going to be a little more difficult to trace ownership of the boat, but nothing was believed impossible. What was possible though was that it would no doubt take time.

Tidal factors were to be considered too. Huws had been told that if there was likelihood that the boat had not actually been motoring prior to having been found as the dead man's handle had been actioned, then consideration to the tidal flow and wind at the time around the island of Anglesey would have to be looked into. The fact that the tide had a unique way of going clockwise for a number of hours before slack water preceded it, then going anti clockwise, meant the Coastguard officers on watch had a fair task on their hands.

Huws said goodbye to Rowlands and thanked him for working late into the night. He left the officers to share a masked drive back to station. The drive home was short, a light had been left on in the hall, he dropped his keys into a glass dish on the table, immediately regretting the metallic clink, imagining that his mother may hear it and use the excuse of hearing a possible break in to her nosey advantage, an opportunity to interrogate him for information. Nobody stirred, not even old Ben, sleeping deep slumber of an elderly contented dog. In the kitchen, his supper sat in the fridge, a note stuck to the door with a Lake District fridge magnet. Instructions to put it in the microwave for six minutes. He smiled, thankful for his mother's kindness, as he scraped it into the bin, hunger long gone, bed was calling.

Chapter Seven

THE OFFICE WAS BUZZING the next morning when Huws arrived, familiar faces from previous enquiries delegated to form a team. All keen and enthusiastic, no one glorified from having a potential murder or three on their patch, but there was a distinct keenness in the atmosphere. A change from the general humdrum of police day-to-day life of following up reports on second home owners sneaking in under the cover of darkness which seemed to be the main avenue of complaints that they had locally currently.

"Right, what have we got, anything? Anybody?" asked Huws, looking around at the general head down hive of activity from his colleagues.

"We're working on the maroon car seen the night of the Coast-guard callout that was in the carpark above white beach," piped up a young female officer.

"There aren't a lot of them registered in that colour, apparently it was some sort of limited edition at the time, but the EL prefix is Essex, so we have found one with the EL42 reg which is registered, taxed, MOT'd and insured in the name of Richard Flint with an address in a village called Colne Engaine near Colchester Essex. We have this morning asked the local Colchester force if they can afford a couple of officers to go and see if he is there. It's likely that he could well have driven there overnight and be sitting at home. We're waiting for a response on that today."

"Good work, I like to see initiative officer. Has anyone contacted the operations centre for the expressway to see if any cameras have picked the car up last night leaving the island via either bridge?" asked Huws. "Maybe worth checking up with the Britannia garage in Menai Bridge or One stop in Llandegai, for a car of that description having topped up with fuel, in fact ask all the A55 garages to check their cameras to be sure".

"I will do that," announced Parry from the back, he had been twiddling his thumbs, not sure what his role could be in his first CID operation. He had his head down and into his laptop quick as a flash. Huws smiled to himself, youthful enthusiasm, preceding, no doubt years down the line, he would become just the same as most of the rest of them, and realise that in general, policing was just routine and on occasions monotonous. A mobile phone rang, its owner chatting away as she typed single handed onto the keyboard in front of her.

"Sir, we have a negative on the whereabouts of the car owner at the moment, he lives in a house on a small housing estate in that village I mentioned, but there is no answer at the door and no car to be seen. A neighbour popped out and said that he had been gone from there for a few days, though she had no idea where he had gone."

Not well liked apparently, a bit of a hot head was how he was described. Always had undesirables visiting him, at all hours of the day and night.

The police say he isn't known to them but could obviously be keeping his nose just clean enough that he is not on the radar. They are going to knock on a few doors in the village, its only small, to see if anyone knows of his whereabouts, but he does warn that the village is a bit of a dormitory, in that most people drive off to the nearest train station first thing, commute London or Chelmsford and return late at night, so not as close knit as you might imagine a village to be."

"Shall I put a description of the car on our Police Facebook page Sir? It may well stir someone's memory locally if they have seen the car around and about too. Would the Coastguard officers who were involved the other day be able to give a description of the man they dealt with; he is likely connected with the body isn't he?" These young officers were certainly on the ball.

Huws wavered at this, he still hadn't got used to there being a Police Facebook presence, especially since it seemed to give voice to a lot of anti- police people, though he did know that every man and his dog now seemed to use social media.

"Good idea son. Have a word with the senior officer in charge in the Coastguard Ops room in Holyhead, they can contact the team members who dealt with him that night. We don't have a positive ID yet on the man in the water, so we can't be sure if he is this Richard man or whether the one who called the coastguard is Richard Flint, that man seems to have disappeared off the face of the earth, but yes, put it on Facebook and see if anything useful comes out of it".

Chapter Eight

HE HAD AWOKEN to sunshine pushing its way in around the edge of the Roman blinds in the small window, he checked his phone, it was only six am. How nice would it just be if he could throw them open and enjoy the view across the field down to the cliff edge ahead. He daren't. He rose with a yawn, a troubled night's sleep behind him, he had to get his sensible head on today and decide the best way forwards out of here. He had seen on the news the night before that three bodies had been recovered off the coast, he knew two of them but other than the confrontation the night before they were found, he had no personal connections or knowledge of the other except that he was known to Ricky's son. He obviously had the same streak of greed running through his centre like a stick of Blackpool rock, as both he and Ricky had.

Already that morning he had decided that he would leave the car somewhere, somewhere convenient that he could then catch a bus to the nearest town with a train station, but whilst there was still a local lockdown and no one likely to turn up at the cottage, he would keep his head down until things had died down locally.

He took a place mat off the pile on the table and opened the self- seal plastic packet that he had in his wallet. He carefully poured the white powder onto the smooth surface and using his credit card he divided it into two clean thin lines. He snorted it hard through the plastic straw that he had found in the kitchen, sitting back in the chair he awaited the Cocaine hit. He knew this didn't last as long as injecting it would have done, but the euphoria and feeling of confidence and self- control he knew it gave him was worth the shortened duration of its effects. It had been a treat to himself when he had grabbed the bag out of Ricky's desperate hands. He hoped it would clarify his plan to escape.

Chapter Nine

"SIR," called Parry from amongst the beavering heads in the room. "It's a negative on the A55 garage CCTV cameras, and the one at the Britannia garage. No car of that description has been seen, but someone who has just seen our Facebook page said that the car was in Llangoed three days ago outside the shop and two men got out of it and went inside. I've got their details off messenger to maybe have a chat with them"?

"Great stuff," responded DS Howard, appearing pleased that their new young sidekick was not too shy to show some initiative, but he had sensed that would be the case anyway.

"Shall I go down to the shop with Parry here and have a chat with them? There may well be a camera in the shop somewhere, because I'm quite sure it is a Post Office as well as a shop, they usually have CCTV for security because of the money kept there, at least our village post office has it at home."

"Yes, lad off you go," said Huws, Parry being on his feet like a startled jack rabbit, grabbing his helmet off the table before the words had entirely left his mouth. "This might tell us whether the man is our victim and also we may get an ID for the other man who called the Coastguard out, one of them may well be Richard Flint."

Huws knew, so far at least, that the man that had called the coastguard could be identified by a couple of the Coastguard team, that the man in the water was a different man, but without a face to the name, it was unknown as yet which was Richard Flint and therefore who was man number two. According to the cameras on both the old bridge and the Britannia a car of the description they had been given by a coastguard team member, had not left the island. A sudden thought occurred to him, dammit why hadn't it struck him before…

"Right, one other thing, can one of you get in contact with the port officers on duty in Holyhead and see if they remember a car of that description getting on a ferry any time after the Coastguard team left the scene at White Beach and check the port entrance cameras. It might actually be worth one of the Holyhead traffic lads having a look around the port car park or any nearby side streets in case he left the car and crossed as a foot passenger. If that's the case, we will likely have little chance of finding him."

Huws kept his cool as he delivered his orders, but he was annoyed with himself for not thinking of this, hours earlier.

A phone call to Rowlands the pathologist was the next call on his list, they had three people in the fridges not just the one, there was no definite link yet between the three, but it nagged at him that both incidents had happened within a few hours of each other, gut feeling told him that they should not discount a link, but, experience had taught him over the years that a link was in no way guaranteed.

He sat down at his desk in the next room, the same old wobbly office chair that he couldn't bear to get rid of. Gwen had bought it for him on his promotion to CID years ago. On the filing cabinet ahead of him, a picture of himself, Gwen, with Elin their daughter and Ben the dog that had been taken on a family outing to walk up the Watkin path to Snowdon's summit, on a beautiful summer's day five years before. A kind walker had offered to take the photo for them. Gwen and Elin smiling and looking relaxed, he, well, he looked flustered and red with exertion. The top section had frightened him to death with its loose scree rolling away under his feet, while Gwen and Elin just strode on like agile mountain goats.

Moments like this glance, had the power to throw him totally off kilter, he was pleased to have work to concentrate on because the thought of being home alone with his thoughts made him afraid it would unleash a torrent of grief that he felt had been kept simmering and suppressed below the surface since her sudden death.

It had been so sudden. To wake in the morning to find Gwen still in bed next to him was in itself unusual. Always the one to be up with the lark with 'things to do'. The moments of first awakening, when thoughts are just transitioning from dreams to reality gave rise to the awareness of silence. A weight in the bed next to him, but silence, total silence. No adjusting of an uncomfortable leg, or movement of an awakening head on a pillow, and no gentle breath sounds. He had slipped his hand slowly across towards Gwen and felt the cotton of her nightdress, she didn't stir at this intrusion, or reach her body towards him in a pre- awakening hug, content and familiar. He reached further and there it was, cold, cold skin.

He knew she was dead before he even sat himself up, he had dealt with enough sudden deaths to know now that the next moments in his actions were going to reveal the worst imaginable reality. Part of him wanted to turn over and return to the secure safe slumber of moments ago, not wanting to fully wake and absorb the truth. What about Elin he thought. She would be just stirring now in the room just across the landing, getting herself ready for a school day ahead. Totally unaware of the horror that had occurred just across the landing.

He flung the quilt back and knelt up on the bed to face Gwen, she had her back to him, lying on her side, he rolled her onto her back and imagined for a split second of abject terror that he may need to attempt to resuscitate her. One look at her face, blue tinged and set, he knew it was too late for that, even the motion of pulling her over indicated she may have been dead for a number of hours. How could he not have noticed, how did he not know she was in trouble, had he maybe not woken when she may have nudged him or called out?

His train of thought was stopped abruptly, by a light knock on the door followed by Elin's entrance, swiftly followed by an excited Ben launching himself onto the bed as he was apt to. Huws had no idea or plan, but Elin realized immediately that something was bad, really bad.

"Your mum is gone, sweetheart."

Elin stood at the end of the bed, Huws had pulled the confused dog away from Gwen and it was in a dreamlike trance that he became aware of screaming in the room, Elin. He could do nothing, he was still on his knees next to Gwen, pathetic in his inactiveness, unable to deal with his bereft confused daughter, unable to cope with himself.

That had up to then been the very worst day of his life, he had rung for an ambulance to come, knowing they could only declare Gwen dead, he knew it would involve a police visit, likely one of his own colleagues because it would be considered a sudden unexpected death.

He had still been barefoot and in his pyjamas when he opened the door to a paramedic, he recognized him too, likely from some incident they had attended together. He was speechless, aimlessly pointing at the staircase. He joined a shivering Elin in the lounge, sobs erupting intermittently from their little girl. He held her close, any words of comfort refusing to leave his lips. How could he comfort her when he himself was broken into a million pieces?

The young policeman sent to survey the scene, briefly popped his head around the lounge door after he had been upstairs. He commiserated with them both, neither of them looking up from their own thoughts, even Ben the dog had not lifted his head at the intrusion of strangers as he sat across Elin's feet, sensing as only dogs can that something major had happened to his human family.

The worst part had been the appearance of the local under-taker, a man well known to Huws through the job, who had placed Gwen's body carefully and with gentleness and great care just as she was, in her nightclothes into a body bag, she was placed onto a lightweight stretcher and he and his black suited assistant had taken her out into his hearse. Sliding her into the compartment under-neath where a coffin would lie.

A couple of the near neighbours were outside their homes, bewildered in what they were witnessing. One neighbor, clearly about to make his way towards Idris Huws, who was in no way ready to accept what had happened let alone talk to anyone. He had turned on his heel and shut his front door after him. This had all been a horrific nightmare, something he had never imagined would have happened at this stage of their lives. He knew the process, the autopsy, the cause of death, all that had to be done. No long retirement years, not being present at Elin's wedding together as proud parents. Not being proud grandparents to any children Elin may have in the future. His future imagined life had been erased and stolen from him in the blink of an eye.

That was then, this was now. He refused to let the pooling tears leave his eyes, he dried his eyes then gave his nose a good blow into his hanky, picking up the phone he dialed his old friend Emyr Rowland's number at the autopsy suite.

Chapter Ten

"HI EMYR, Idris, any more information on the two boatmen that may connect them to the other body?"

"Nothing, unfortunately. The only suggestion that I have is that we let Jane here work her magic and get a couple of presentable photographs that you can release to the press and see if that nudges someone's conscience or recognition."

"Right you are, I'll leave that to you to sort, send us the photos when you've got them. In my experience, people only step forwards when the people in the photos are goodies as opposed to baddies, time will no doubt tell with this incident," answered Huws.

Stepping out into the corridor not totally concentrating, he crashed full on into by the ever- enthusiastic PC Parry.

"Sorry Sir, we had a chat with the shopkeeper, they did have cameras and I have the disc ready to put into my laptop to have a look through. Two men he said, reasonably tall and well built, one matching the description of our body in the water, the other wearing an old grubby waxed jacket, jeans, and walking or work type boots, scruffy, unshaven looking, an unhealthy pallor and hair that looked as if it hadn't seen a comb or a pair of clippers for a while. London type accents he recalls or southern at least. They bought a carrier bag full of food. Interestingly the scruffy one turned a bit defensive with him when he asked them if they were staying local, considering most holiday cottages are closed and second home owners encouraged not to travel. He knows most of the locals, even if they didn't come into the shop as he lives in the village anyway."

Parry had his head down in his pocket book, Huws could see that he had almost written an essay, he smiled to himself. Keen.

Parry continued- "he said that their attitude and rudeness had slightly shocked him, and he actually went to the door to see where they had gone. That's when he saw the car, the bearded man was driving and they drove off at a fair lick down the hill towards the bridge, he said he obviously couldn't see which way they had gone at the bottom, whether they had turned left for Glanrafon or gone straight on. A couple of people came into the shop a few minutes later who live at the bottom of the hill so they might well have seen the car. We got their name and address and popped to see them, both of them said the car had gone straight over the bridge and up towards Cornelyn. They could have turned left or right at the junction though, but if you do turn left you would be able to continue then turn right for White beach."

Parry stopped, and Huws could have sworn he had taken a bit of a gasp for breath. He hadn't paused throughout his report.

"Good work Parry, useful information, I will have a word with DS Howard and go on from here."

"Uhm Sir, I was thinking, you had us checking the A55 cameras for cars leaving the island, should we maybe have checked the west bound cameras too incase we can see them coming onto it, particularly on the day of the incident?" Parry added. He had a good officer in the making here thought Huws, "Yes, yes, you can get on with that now after you have written up your report from your visit. Ask one of the more experienced team members to look over it before you upload it to the system. It has to be spot on."

"Yes Sir, will do." He seemed quite pleased with himself.

He stepped outside into the late summer afternoon, Howard, at his request had followed him outside.

"I'm going to take a few hours off this afternoon, I will touch base with you again this evening, I've a couple of errands to do. Keep an eye on Parry, hopefully we may get a camera spot of the car coming onto the island. Chase up the lads at the Port and see if they've got anything for us. We might also, before the end of the day get a couple of photos from Jane at the autopsy suite, she was going to try to get some images of how the two boat men would have looked so we can release the photos maybe to the National press and even to the TV News. Apparently, there have already been a few press phone calls coming in."

"Sir," Howard nodded, "We'll do our best."

Chapter Eleven

IDRIS HUWS PUT the key in the door of his 'antique' car with a hint of a smile. He got in, sinking into the soft leather, bottom encapsulating seat, the edge nearest the door now well-worn from years of brushing against various coats. He was positive that there was a bum shaped dip in the leather by now after all these years. The old leather cover on the steering attached, by its crisscrossing long thin leather lace by his father years ago was hot against his hands, having been in the full glare of the afternoon sun.

Sitting in this car bought back memories of family beach picnics, the dog in the boot, or the many camping holidays they had taken over the years until Elin started to get 'bored' as many teenagers claimed to become. She had still enjoyed their hill walks over on the mainland, right up until shortly before Gwen's death. He imagined that Gwen would have been so frustrated now at the ' no exercising away from home' guideline- at not being able to drive down to the Llyn peninsular walking the headlands and coves around Tydweiliog, one of their favourite places to sit and watch the sun go down to the west, with the seals bottling in the sea below them, a term which Elin had educated him about. Ben the dog would silently watch out for them whilst his whole body quivered in excitement and anticipation.

His earlier 'wobble' in the privacy of his office had shaken him today more than usual. The vivid recollection of those awful moments hitting him like a wielded club. On the few occasions it had happened, it had taken his breath away as if it was happening again right in front of him.

One of his friends, had a while ago suggested he might want to get some counselling; thoughtful of them, but he was never keen on that. Always quick to suggest it to his colleagues, but not admitting to having his own need. Mind you, lockdown and the whole COVID-19 business seemed to have put paid to it anyway. No one seemed to want to be in contact with anyone else if it could be in any way avoided, being a tech- dinosaur he had also avoided at all costs the zoom meetings which were all the rage nowadays. Thankfully they were rare in his profession. He would sort himself out given time. Most people who knew him fully believed that he was 'over' his loss, when in reality it was simply well hidden.

He turned the key in the ignition, always grateful that the engine started sweetly at every attempt, never yet letting him down. He swung left out of the police compound and made his way out of the small town towards a place that hurt him so much to visit. Stopping at the garage in Pentraeth he picked up a bunch of flowers, knowing that Gwen had always teased him for buying her flowers at a garage, and made his way on to the peaceful little graveyard where her body had been laid to rest.

There was never anyone here when he visited, he was always glad of this, to be able to speak to Gwen with no earwigging, gave him a moment of much needed comfort. Sometimes the intense need to speak to her overwhelmed him, such seemed its urgency. There was no stone on her grave yet, it was all organized and paid for, but the stonemason had advised leaving the ground to settle first to allow for subsidence. It made him feel a little neglectful, it was a fact that he had never needed to know until last year. A huge part of him still couldn't comprehend that her body was six feet or so down in the sun warmed earth at his feet. He occasionally sat on the nearby low boundary wall to 'chat' but thought it a little unbecoming in a graveyard. Coming here simply made the whole loss real.

He worried about ridiculous unspoken things, for instance would she have been displeased to have been buried in a nighty bought urgently days after her death for the single purpose of burial, as opposed to some sensible normal day to day clothing. He shook his head at the ridiculousness of his bizarre thoughts. Should she have been given some nice shoes.

He pulled at the few weeds that were growing through the summer cracked soil, realising the futility of it, when in fact grass growth on the cracked soil needed encouraging to hide the excavation. He said a muttered goodbye and placed the plastic wrapped bunch of flowers at the foot of the wooden cross with Gwen's name on, kindly supplied to mark the grave by the undertaker. A daft thought crossed his mind, he was pleased that she would have known her direct grave occupant neighbours on either side. Random thoughts.

He knew her death had made him a bit selfish, no one else's death seemed as bad and deserving of sympathy as Gwen's, even the three bodies they were dealing with now, hadn't produced a single thought of sadness in him. He really didn't care. The death of a person so close to you could do that, he found.

He drove home through the village and turned into the drive, looking up for a moment at the same house, the same curtains, the same flowers in the same pots that had regrown from Gwen's previous efforts, growing through the remnants of last summer's old leaves, unpruned, but no Gwen to welcome him in.

As he put his key in the door, he could already hear the clacketing of Ben's excited feet on the laminate floor of the hallway. He, at least, was always pleased to see him home.

There was no immediate sign of his mother when he went through to the kitchen, but he could smell a meal in preparation in the oven. She could be seen taking clothes off the line through the kitchen window. He was truly in one sense, grateful for her doing these chores as God knows how he would have coped otherwise looking after himself and a maturing, and on occasion now difficult, daughter.

Things had slightly improved between his mother and himself when there had been a few fireworks, he came home one day to find some family photos removed and put in a drawer, 'because they were upsetting,' had been her apologetic excuse. She had been told firmly that evening that this was still Gwen's house. He had felt the need to apologise the next day for his outburst, but he was unsure how, when all the lockdowns ended and COVID-19 was hopefully behind them he was going to broach the subject of her returning to her own home.

Chapter Twelve

HIS HEAD WAS in a bit of a fug when he had come down from his hit. It never lasted long when he snorted, but it was better than nothing. He was however, no nearer finalizing his plan to get away. He needed to keep his head down in case of repercussions, but he was also quite confident that the delivery arrangements had been made through Ricky so hopefully no link to him. He had been tempted earlier to try to make his way across the fields from the cottage to pick up the gun but had thought better of it. He opened the packet of back bacon and set it under the grill. At least he would not go hungry for a couple of days, even if the shopping bag didn't really contain much of any substance. Just a load of quickly grabbed junk food.

Outside, unseen because of the closed curtains prowled a neighbour. A neighbour who had been asked by the cottage owner to keep an eye on the closed- up cottage. He was surprised today to find a car around the back. He was even more surprised to smell the wafting enticing aroma of bacon through the extractor fan vent. Luck was on the side of the cottage incumbent, that he neither had the key with him or the bravery to apprehend any wrongdoer. He left by the garden gate as silently as he had entered.

The bacon sandwich was enjoyed; however, satisfying his hunger had clarified his need to retrieve the gun.

A local OS map laminated and framed on the wall showed clearly that if he walked a couple of hundred yards back up the road from his dead-end location, he could pick up the coastal path again to White beach, hopefully without coming across any other people. He washed his face, a bleary-eyed tired, drawn looking person staring back at him from the bathroom mirror. His bloodshot eyes still showing a Cocaine dilation. A sure giveaway for someone educated in these matters.

He put some water on his disheveled locks, which at least flattened them down and once he ran his comb through it, he thought he looked like a slicked back hair- styled east end gangster. He had never thought of himself in those terms until a couple of days ago. It made him feel quite smart, or maybe that was just the remnants of the stimulating effects of the coke he had taken.

He grabbed his coat, and left by the back door, leaving it unlocked for his return. Striding down the road, he tried his best to look like any other local walker out for a breath of air. He hoped he wouldn't get lost on his route across the clifftops.

"Can't be that difficult," he said out loud to himself. He passed a string of houses along the few hundred metres until the coastal path sign indicated his route to the right. He had kept his head down along the road, walking purposely lest anyone was outdoors and engaged with him. The track was rough underfoot, but good attempts to lay a boardwalk made his progress easier. He was well off the road in no time at all. He hoped he could find the gun quickly so as to not spend too much time in the open.

Chapter Thirteen

"GOOD EVENING SIR, sorry to disturb you," came DS Howard's voice on the mobile.

"It's ok, I was about to touch base shortly. Do we have any more information?" Huws got off the sofa, to walk to the kitchen, changing his mind he went out through the front door, on noticing his mother laboriously heaving herself out of her armchair, no doubt to follow him. He doubted she would ever learn. "Sorry, had to step outside. What is it?"

"Some interesting information from the local station in Menai Bridge. A member of the public was going to report a Covid lockdown breach possibly taking place in a cottage not far from Caim, Penmon. He had however contacted the owner whose number he had. Turns out they are not at the cottage, no one booked in to stay there because of lockdown regulations. The officer I spoke to assumed there may be a break in, or squatter situation, however, what is of interest to us is that the maroon Octavia is parked out of sight around the back. It's unlikely there are two of that colour locally. The guy didn't think to get a reg number, but I'm getting a team together to go there, including the firearms team which is what we are waiting for at the moment".

"Excellent work, I'll make my way there as quickly as I can." Already back in the hallway grabbing his car key and coat, ignoring his mother who had clearly been earwigging behind the door as he had almost splatted her into the wall in his door opening ferocity.

"Yes Sir, but please hold back at the nearby junction to wait for the firearms team, there isn't a lot of room to park there. I have also asked for helicopter back up too; they should be over shortly in case whoever it is does a runner. We will lose light soon unfortunately, but they will pick up someone running, quicker than we will with their thermal imaging cameras. We are assuming it's our man from the other night that the Coastguard dealt with and assume now he was connected to the body." Added Howard, concern audible in his voice.

"Yes, yes, I'll wait." If only Howard realized how little thought DI Huws had for his own safety.

He got in the car, Elin came to the door, he opened the window and declared that it was work and hopefully he wouldn't be long. She lifted her hand and her eyebrow in disdain, more than likely at him leaving her with her grandmother for yet another evening. He was still uncomfortable granting permission for her to stay out later with friends. The only advantage of lockdown that he could see, the controlling of meeting in groups.

He knew the way to the location, the back lanes from his village familiar to him. The roads were quiet, as they had indeed been through this strange time of pandemic in the countryside. He made progress quickly to the junction. Swiftly joined by DS Howard and his new sidekick Parry. Parry was out of the car and donning his cap before the engine had stopped. Huws did notice that he had swapped his helmet for the North Wales police issue CID baseball cap.

"I didn't know you were on duty this evening Parry?" asked Huws.

"I wasn't Sir, but I didn't want to miss out on something involving this case, Llangefni said it was ok for me to come," he said.

"Surely there must be a young lady waiting for you at home, annoyed that you have run out on her for work."

"Man," responded Parry quick as a flash. "My partner is a man."

"Right, you are," said Huws, this was the norm now and who was he to judge. Nothing he came across surprised him anymore.

"Young man then. Hope he appreciates the life of a policeman these days, especially a policeman keen on getting onto the CID team where there are no timetables or shifts at all during a job. We take our breaks when we can."

"Oh, he certainly does, he is in the job himself, understands the score fully." Parry smiled. "Don't worry, just like a working Straight police couple, we don't let our relationship affect our work." Huws chose to change the subject at this point, the less he knew of the intricacies of his officers lives the better as far as he was concerned. He had not really required the detail delivered.

"Do we have any information of a time to scene of the armed lads? I don't want to make way to this cottage before we have them here." He looked up at this point as he heard the whirring of the helicopter rotors approach from the direction of the Great Orme. "Get the ops room to tell the helicopter crew to stand off for a while will you, we don't want to alert whoever may be in the cottage that something is kicking off. As far as I can be sure, there will be a clear eye of sight for miles in every direction almost from the front window of that particular cottage placed where it is."

"Right on it Sir," said Howard, already dialing his phone. Parry wearing his conventional radio and earpiece stated that the armed response vehicle was approximately two minutes away and a couple of squad cars were right behind them.

The people of Caim must no doubt wonder what on earth was going on just up the road in their normally sleepy hamlet.

Chapter Fourteen

HE ARRIVED BACK at the cottage as the day was just taking on the dark red and orange glow of the sunset displaying to the west. He had found the gun easily despite having just lobbed it out of hand. He realised he was lucky that not many people walked the paths, as no doubt anyone may have noticed the gunmetal glisten when the sun got through the brambles to it. Luck was clearly on his side. He felt more confident now he had it by his side again. He was still unsure whether there would be repercussions from the incident. He knew however that Ricky had not actually been to the cottage before they had made their way to the pick- up point. Hopefully that meant that anyone else that Ricky had let in on the plan would have to actually find him first. He wasn't sure whether Ricky would have been stupid enough to do that, in fact, he was so greedy, he wouldn't have wanted to share his cut any thinner than necessary.

He abandoned the back bedroom for now, lulled into a sense of security that he reminded himself was no way guaranteed. Almost treating the place as if he was actually enjoying a holiday.

The television was on quietly, the news already telling him that the incident was now out there in the public domain. There had also been a description of his car plastered all over the Welsh news channel. It had been Ricky's idea to come up here, saying it was quiet, and as long as they travelled up across country along the old A5 route, it was likely that there was less risk of any cameras picking them up. All he knew now was that he was a hell of a long way from home in an area unfamiliar to him, with no easy exit plan. He knew the nearest station was likely Bangor, or that place on the island with the daft long name, but how he would get to either unnoticed was something he still hadn't worked out.

He would Google the train time tables shortly, maybe an early morning train would be best, allowing him to leave the cottage before anyone else might be around. He had been aware of occasional voices, as people walked past the gable of the cottage and through the gate into the field but maybe at crack of dawn, he would be ok to leave. He thought about the bags of coke he still had in his pocket, but his head was too full of plans at the moment to allow him the luxury of another hit. That could wait. He had lots more where that had come from.

Chapter Fifteen

EVERYONE WAS IN PLACE, the police negotiator from HQ was there with his loudhailer, another with the ever useful but damaging Ram as well as a couple of trained officers with their SG516 semi-automatics. Huws hated to see these and had already instructed the officers to not use them, unless there was no other option, and only then shoot to injure. Huws stood back behind the main line.

Howard and Parry retreated to the far side of the cottage in the field. Not just to be out of the way, but to immediately block the path of any walkers, who might appear innocently from somewhere, though it was now increasingly unlikely in the darkening evening.

"Whoever is inside, come out with your hands up in front of you, we are giving you this opportunity to show yourself before we come in."

Huws had only a couple of times in his service been in this position, but it still sent a shiver down his back to hear these sorts of commands. He hoped whoever it was would just come out of his own accord, everyone then could just go home with no more than that order given.

They waited, the shout was repeated this time declaring a countdown, 10, 9 ....3,2,1 the command to use the ram immediately followed. No messing with these chaps thought Huws, as he saw an officer give the first impact. Pity about the door, but then needs must. The occupier if indeed he was there at all had been given his chance.

Suddenly gunshots, two. A shout for help. Huws thought for a minute that the Ram wielding officer had been shot, but no the desperate shouting was now coming from around the back of the cottage, his heart thudded in his chest as he recognized the shouts as DS Howard.

"Shit, get round there," he shouted at the armed officer nearest him, "now!" His own feet instinctively running in the same direction, another officer saying that the helicopter had picked up a figure making for the deer park wall to their right, that they'd try to keep him in their view. The sight in front of him was one he had hoped never to see. Howard bent over a blood covered Parry, screaming at him to respond, "Get an ambulance crew here now!" he screamed, "Help him."

Huws could hear all this and see it all playing like a horror film in front of his eyes. He was rigid with uselessness. Incapable, shocked at his own inaction. One of the firearms officers was seemingly pushing both his hands deep into Parry's abdomen, attempting to staunch the thick red blood oozing from around his fingers.

Parry's eyes were open, terror and bewildered surprise, in equal measure. Bright red blood was bubbling its way out of his mouth and down his chin, soaking into the collar of his shirt, spreading like an ugly pattern, growing and wet. Huws shook himself out of his nightmare vision, he knelt down and grabbed Parry's hand, his colleagues busy now trying to stop the bleeding.

"You'll be fine lad, don't you worry. We'll get you sorted out, two minutes, the ambulance will be here, you wait and see. You will look back at this when you are a DI and realise what a baptism of fire you will have had in CID. Hold on now lad."

Parry gurgled through the blood, frothing now in big bubbles from his airways, Huws held his hand tight.

"Hang on in there, son". These words came out of his mouth as Parry took an open- mouthed desperate hungry gasp for air, and another, he saw the life leave the young officer's eyes. All the ambition, all the enthusiasm, keenness, youth, a future, just gone as if a light switch had been pulled.

Howard jumped to his chest and started delivering desperate compressions, swiftly eased away by the shoulders by the other officer. An experienced officer, realising that the catastrophic blood loss meant that their efforts here in the field would already have been futile, such was the damage to his abdomen and chest. Huws stood above him, looking down, deeply shocked, transfixed by the sight before him. Howard unashamedly sobbed and rocked back on his heels and screamed into the cooling evening air.

"You bastard, you absolute fucking bastard. We will get you if it's the last thing I will do in this job. I know you can probably hear me, you shitty worthless scumbag coward, we will find you." Howard was being pulled to his feet by one of the armed officers.

"Come on mate, let's get you away from here, the rest of the team will get on with the task of finding whoever did this, we can talk about what happened later back at the station".

Howard was sobbing, great big snotty nosed gasps, he looked towards Huws. "I loved him Sir, more than anything in the world, and he has been taken away from me like someone blowing out a match." Huws did something then that he had never done before as an officer, he stepped towards Howard and embraced him tight. To hell with Covid. One thing was for sure, he knew exactly what this young man feeling at this moment in time. He had no words of consolation, he understood full well that at this point in time they would have no meaning whatsoever for him.

Chapter Sixteen

THERE WAS no going back now, he had truly pissed on his chips, as his old dad used to say each time, he managed to get involved with yet another doomed illegal plan to make his fortune. He had blown it. If only the two officers had not been standing there just as he made it out of the window and across the garden.

As soon as he had reached the picket- fence he had seen them and they him. The first uniformed officer had made a move towards him and he'd raised his gun without thinking, instinct and fear making him pull the trigger twice, full frontal. The poor bugger didn't have a chance. Luckily for him the other officer had dealt with his colleague and ignored him. He had made his way through a metal kissing gate and had run in the shadow of a high wall and across the field towards what seemed to be some sort of church building. He kept to the right, hiding inside a Church would be just too obvious, he crossed the track by what seemed to be some sort of pay booth, and around the edge of another building he found a track which seemed to take him down towards the sea. It was only at this point that he could hear the helicopter which was obviously back across the field at the cottage. He had miraculously made good distance despite being completely unfit and flabby around the edges. The ground was leg breakingly rough, winter- tractor created mud ruts, hardened by summer heat into concrete like ridges. He would be lucky to get to the shore without falling. He was blowing like he had never blown before, zilch fitness, but dependent on the adrenaline coursing through his body, his heart however, he imagined was going to leap out of his chest.

Through another metal gate he went. He was aware now that there were cattle alongside him in the field, could be to his advantage. There was a building to his right, a padlocked door, but to his left there appeared to be some tunnel entrances, three or four of them, he grabbed his phone and put the torch on. Knee deep in dry cow muck but built into the hillside. This would take the heat off the chase just for now and give him breathing space. Literally in the sense of both words, get his breath back, and if the helicopter as likely had a heat seeking device on it, it may well not penetrate through the depth of earth and brickwork above him. Curious cattle were approaching him now, he was fine with that. Another warmth giving creature to confuse the heat seeker. He snorted his breath in with a laugh, how had he suddenly developed the brains to work such things out. But one thing was for sure, he had killed a cop now to add to his tally, they would hunt him to the ends of the earth now. He was in serious trouble.

There was also another issue that he needed to contend with. The package containing some of the money and heroin was under the spare tyre in the boot of the car. Thankfully the larger share he had stuffed in his pockets. Had all his efforts been a total waste? He hoped not. To that thought, he punched the bricked wall of the tunnel with a ferocity from inside that cut his knuckles almost to their bones. He silently mouthed his tirade of expletives, still conscious that there would be a search party out for him, he shook his hand, and wiped his own blood onto his thigh, having no hanky at his disposal. What to do now was the question, could he continue unseen under the cloak of darkness, or should he just hunker down here? Two of the inquisitive cows were currently blocking his exit, and being a townie, he didn't fancy his chances pushing them out of the way. He would stay put just for now, maybe in a while the helicopter would need to refuel.

Chapter Seventeen

HUWS HAD DESPERATELY WANTED to drive Howard home himself, but knew he now had a major search to organize. He had directed one of the young female officers on the team to drive him home and stay with him. He had asked the police surgeon to take a look at him with a view of possibly giving him a light sedative, but it had been refused. Howard was dumbstruck, barely able to utter a single word.

One job he would have to do with absolute haste was to drive to Parry's parent's home and break the news. Their address had been on his file. It was a while since he himself had delivered an agony message as they called them, not since he was a Police Sergeant had he carried out that particular task. A job he hated, and certainly the first since losing Gwen, he wasn't even sure if he could do this without breaking down himself, so fragile was his own emotional state. But do it he must.

The uniformed lads were being briefed in the incident room across the hall. The helicopter as yet not having found anything, in itself strange, considering he couldn't have been a million miles away, but he knew time had been lost when they had quite rightly been dealing with Parry with the helicopter still on standby just out at sea, awaiting the go ahead.

He knew the search would spread out like the spokes of a wheel from the cottage, they were also painfully aware that very likely he was still armed.

The Octavia had been removed to the garages behind the station, a local recovery truck asked to remove it on a suitable trailer. Maybe, just maybe they would glean some information from that.

Huws knew he was procrastinating now. He needed to get going to Waunfawr on the mainland to pay his visit. He was dreading it. As per normal in these circumstances he had asked a female officer to accompany him. Neither he nor anyone else had seen their beds yet since the incidents. All running on anger and adrenaline. Dawn had broken into a beautiful day which belied the darkness that over-shadowed everyone's thoughts and sorrow.

What a morning this was turning out to be. As he left his office, he was pleased to see a centipede of officers leaving the building, all now prepped as to what their task was to be. He hoped to God the day wouldn't end with another death. He was however now aware that the order was, 'shoot to kill' if it became necessary, an order never made lightly, and a long time since the North Wales police had been given such an order. His mind took him back to a tale his late father told him of a search he had been involved with in 1961, when a policeman colleague had been shot in the face and blinded by the person they were chasing. In those days there was no armed unit and certainly no bullet proof clothing. He put his head around the door of the incident room, mumbled an, "Are you ready?" towards the female officer and strode off to where he had parked his car early hours.

The whole incident from arriving at the cottage to seeing Parry off in the undertaker's black transit, etched behind his eyeballs. He was not looking forwards to the next couple of hours.

Chapter Eighteen

HE HAD MADE the decision at around 1 a.m. that if he was going to make a run for it, he would need to be gone, another few hours and the sun would start to rise, and it would be too late. His phone battery was down to 30%, he needed to at least be able to use the mapping app. Keeping the sea to his left- hand side however had been the obvious choice. He wasn't sure as yet regarding the state of the tide, was it on its way in or out? He ploughed on and it wasn't long before he had come across an old jetty, a farm house stood back from the shore, there had been no lights, it appeared derelict, but he had chosen to keep out onto the sand. There had been no sign of a helicopter or any other traffic on the road above to the right.

The sand was deep and wet, a mixture of mud and sand. He hoped that there wasn't any actual quicksand. That would be just his sort of luck it seemed. He also knew that in the grand scheme of things he didn't deserve any luck. Five lives lost because of him, none intended. Well, not intentionally. If he hadn't been pressurized, that wasn't his fault.

He had walked on around a headland, and along a sandy beach, houses and boathouses to his right, all in darkness. Passing a car parking area, empty at this time of night, apart from one which was distinctly misted up, it's occupants no doubt having more fun than he was at that moment. Slow progress, the tide was encroaching now, he had got his feet wet crossing a river outlet and been forced to scramble up a bank into a field as the water threatened to engulf him. All the time he was thinking of how he might hide his body heat should the helicopter appear again. He continued making slow progress as an edge of orange light started to appear on top of the hills across on the mainland. He needed to find somewhere suitable to hide out fairly quickly.

Chapter Nineteen

HOWARD HAD TAKEN to his bed, curled up like a small child, fully clothed. Totally cried out to the point of exhaustion, stunned, but too shocked to sleep. He was aware that Sarah his colleague was now in the sitting room, 'leaving him to get some sleep,' Two cold cups of tea sat on the bedside table, a skin slowly forming on their surface. Sarah, unsure how to talk to him, aware nothing she could say could make him feel any better, had chosen to sit quietly, deep in her own thoughts.

Howard was painfully aware that he was a grown man, a police officer and that he should simply by job expectation be in control of himself. Nothing had prepared him for this. His mate, his best friend, his lover, his everything, had been wiped out of his life in just a few minutes. How could he go on? Did he even want to go on? At this moment in time, he didn't care what happened to him. He lay shivering and huddled, shutting out the world.

Huws was in virtually the same exact position in the front room of the tidy old farmhouse in Waunfawr. Parry's shocked parents sat holding each other in stoic silence. No doubt the tears would come later. Two cups of tea chilling and untouched on the little table that PC Richards had pulled out of the mahogany nest in the corner.

Virtually a mirror image of Justin Howard's bedside cabinet a few miles away on the island.

A photo of Parry and proud parents at a University Graduation, Bangor he imagined, and a second of the three of them at Parry's passing out parade. An only child he assumed. Mrs. Parry in a summer dress beaming with happiness, Mr. Parry slightly more composed, dignified, but no doubt impressed by his only son, his now late son's achievement. A white toothed smile shining out of Steffan that almost equaled the bulled shine of his parade boots.

He had explained what had happened, cutting out all the detail that they did not need to hear, to haunt their every living moment from that day on. He told them their son was a hero, maybe not in the true sense of the word, but certainly in the future they could take some comfort from his words.

They were pleased that he had not been alone when he died. Huws told them that DS Justin Howard had been by his side as had he himself till the very end. Not a jot of recognition at Howard's name crossed their faces.

The mother spoke first. Huws had learnt over the years that silence was sometimes the best approach once the news was broken. It gave people a chance to form their thoughts and questions before they found the strength to speak. Sometimes there was only silence. Words an agony to voice.

She was sad that his young life had been cut short. He had always wanted to be in the police force, working hard at school and university. Offered a graduate entry at police training school, but he had been determined to start at the bottom and work his way up. They told Huws that he was Steffan's idol, he wanted to be a DI just like Huws, a kind considerate, clever man, she smiled at this, no doubt noticing the kind man opposite squirming slightly in embarrassment at this glorifying. She was sad, they would not see him married to a nice young lady or have him bring children to visit. She shook her head as her husband hugged her closer. Huws doubted that hugging was on the agenda often in this relationship, but situations like this pulled a couple together.

Again, no mention of Howard, thought Huws, Richards looked

across at him. He gave an almost indiscernible shake of his head in the hope that she would recognize the need not to mention the connection with Howard.

Everyone had a right to their secrets.

Huws had asked if there was anyone else, they could ring to come over to them, but the suggestion had been shaken away.

"We will be all right as we are, thank you. We need time alone now. I will phone my brother in a while; Guto here has no family."

Mrs. Parry got to her feet. "Thank you for coming to tell us face to face, but we would like to be alone please if that is ok?" More a statement than a question. Huws and Richards stood. Huws took their hand in turn and squeezed, knowing exactly how the next period of their lives would unfold over the following few hours and days. Changed beyond recognition for the rest of their lives. Incidents like this in his experience often led to a rapid downturn in health and relationships.

A blur of phone calls to the undertaker of choice, a visit by a quietly spoken stranger to discuss, coffins, and wreaths, headstones and grave plots. Something parents should never have to do for their children. He handed Mrs. Parry a card with his own number on it.

"If there is anything we can do regards the funeral arrangements, please let us know, Steffan was very well liked and respected amongst his colleagues, he would have gone far in the force." Head down he left.

Richards slipped into the passenger seat next to him and cried her eyes out, barely having maintained composure as they exited the house. Had he been alone, he may well have done the same. He slid his hand across and lay it on her arm.

"Thank you," she said. "That was so awful, so sad. Those poor people. Poor Justin, they obviously know nothing about the relationship. They obviously don't even know he was gay. Hell, we didn't know he was gay and we worked with him and Justin every day and hadn't twigged that he they were partners. They were both so professional.

Chapter Twenty

A HUSH DESCENDED as he entered the incident room, knowing full well now that the atmosphere within the team would have changed. Yesterday they were looking for the whereabouts of a stranger for a possible link to three deaths, today there would be a new determination, having lost one of their own.

Huws felt it was his job to have a heartfelt, personal chat with the team, they were hurting. Under their perceived tough exteriors, they were humans with feelings like anyone else, despite what the criminal fringe thought of them. Silent tears were spilled in the next ten minutes, composure crumpled for the duration.

They talked of Steffan, they had all liked him, his keenness to do a good job, his intelligence, his sense of humour, his obsession with his hair, his loss to the team in the future. No one had known of his relationship with Justin Howard, but other than mild surprise no one was particularly bothered. Its how things were these days thought Huws.

"Right, are we any further now with all of this. I understand a thorough search is underway in the locality which will gradually be extended through the day. We are assuming the perpetrator is now on foot. We don't know if he is familiar with the area, if he is that's to our disadvantage. We have refused at this point the offer of help from the coastguard service and the RNLI for shore searches, only because we believe he may still be armed. That decision may well be overturned if that belief changes. Any results from a search of the car? Also are we in a position yet to be able to release a photofit out to the public of the gunman, and if possible, the two men in the boat."

He thought he had covered everything, he just paused to receive a mug of coffee off young Richards when, eyes turned to the door and in walked Justin Howard, his face was the colour of the pale wall behind him, eyes darkened and swollen.

"What the hell are you doing here?" demanded one of the team, aghast at his unexpected appearance. "You don't need to be here, take yourself home."

"I wanted to come in, home isn't home now, you obviously know by now that Steffan and I were together as we have been for five years. No one knew, we kept it quiet, Steffan didn't think his mum and dad would be accepting of it. So, it was just between the two of us and it worked well like that. Now I just want to find the bastard that has done this to him and get him behind bars, so please?" he looked at Huws. "Please let me work, it's no help to me whatsoever to be sitting by myself at home, I can't bear the silence."

Huws nodded. "If you're sure, it's what you want to do then who am I to tell you otherwise? Get to your desk, we are just about to catch up with what we have up to now."

"Thank you, Sir."

Howard took off his jacket and pulled the chair away from his desk and opened his laptop. Huws would need to keep an eye on him. Small things, he knew from experience, were quite likely to knock him off kilter.

A disheveled officer stood up with his file of papers in his hand, asked for permission to get Huws up to speed on their work that morning. Huws nodded.

"Good to see you Justin mate, we are all so sorry for your loss, you know we are at the other end of a phone any time day or night."

He cleared his throat looking across at a glassy eyed Justin. He went on to attach a blown-up photograph of two men on the board.

"These are the two men we had on CCTV, one of them we know, is the man that was in the water at White beach. We believe now that he suffered a fatal head injury before he was then likely manhandled and pushed off the edge of the slabs. Unfortunately for his killer, his belt got caught around underwater remains of concrete strengthening rods from the old jetty. Now it seems that the killer had somehow suffered an injury during the scuffle and actually called the coastguard who helped him to the roadway above the cliff. He then refused further help and made his own way from there. Whether he is still carrying this injury we don't know, but it might well slow him down. Maybe the story of being down there fishing was a convenient cover story.

So, having found a driving license in a wallet in the centre cubby in the car, we now know that our victim was Richard Flint from a small village in rural Essex. A bit of a loner by all accounts, not known to involve himself with the villagers, but known by his neighbours to have what they called undesirables visiting.

He also matches CCTV camera footage from the shop in Llangoed."

He pinned the second enhanced picture up on the board next to the first. "This man, we believe is the killer. He was with Richard Flint in the shop and having spoken briefly this morning with two local coastguard officers, they confirm that this was the man they helped up the slope."

He looked around, Justin was staring intently at a spot somewhere on the wall to his left, clearly unable to look at the pictures.

"You ok son?" asked Huws.

"Yes Sir, I don't need to look at the picture. That face will be etched into my memory forever."

The discussion went on. Forensics were also still at the cottage, finding any fingerprints or possible DNA leads that may lead us to the guy. That being only possible if he was already registered on the National Database. If he had kept himself under the radar, they may have nothing to go on.

The next photos to appear were the ones that Jane had managed to produce of the two boatmen. A cracking job she had done too. No one would have guessed that both had been dead at the time the photos were taken. These were now to be released to the national press alongside the photos of the fugitive who was out there somewhere playing cat and mouse.

It was important to stress locally that he should not be approached in any way. No heroics. He was likely armed and highly dangerous with not a care for anyone other than himself. Maybe a few exposures on national news would bring some recognition.

The news on the car was a mixed bag of good and bad. There had been a large amount of heroin found in the floor space under the spare tyre. There had also been a large package of money, a hundred thousand pounds it transpired. Not quite the value of the drugs, but certainly a profit for someone selling it. Was this a drug deal that had gone wrong? Certainly, it was likely to have gone wrong for one person. If they could link the men on the boats to the runaway, then this was a very ambitious drug deal indeed. They may also be in luck, if the killer does not actually have any money on their person, having made a hasty retreat out through the window.

Chapter Twenty-One

HE HAD MANAGED to make his way along the shore bit by bit, trying to keep out of the public gaze as much as he could. There were more people around at the moment, but no one seemed particularly interested in him- yet. He might just get to the station after all, if luck was on his side.

As the day got busier, he had made his way across the road when he came to a garage at the end of town. A gap in a wall to his right a little further on had allowed him to make his way upwards through some undergrowth, until he came to what looked like an old disused track.

He found a likely spot to hide behind an old wall, this would do until dusk fell. He was quite certain that in the hours he had been on the move he had covered a fair bit of ground. Through gaps in the trees below him he could see the pier on the opposite shore seeming to stretch its way almost across the width of the water. He was unsure of his geography and hadn't a clue whether this was the sea or a river. He wondered if there was any possibility at all of getting directly across without arousing suspicion. For now, however, things would have to wait. He was ravenously hungry and now that his adrenaline levels had subsided, he felt he just needed to get his head down for a while and have a snooze.

Chapter Twenty-Two

HUWS HAD POPPED over to the cottage in Caim when he had done everything needed in the office. It was a sit and wait job now to see if anything came of the release of photos to the news channels.

Pictures of the man who was at large were uploaded quickly onto Facebook and Twitter by the media bods. He deemed it of upmost importance to get it out there locally to warn people. This was a highly dangerous individual. Teams of armed officers had never been witnessed walking the back streets of Beaumaris in his time at least. Great consternation and anxiety abounded in local residents.

The cottage owners were on scene when he arrived, full of concern, primarily at not being allowed entry. They had driven from their home in West Sussex when a cottage neighbour had phoned them with the shocking news. They were placated by the fact that there was not much damage other than broken window panes around the back and the front door. An easy fix. The wife was however claiming that the place would never feel the same again after this incident, needlessly adding about the 'poor young police-man' shot just the other side of the garden fence.

"Very unfortunate, and tragic for all concerned," said Huws, hoping that this topic of conversation would come to an abrupt end. He wasn't in the frame of mind to discuss the subject, especially with a distinct feeling the lady was fishing for gossip, a little like his own mother.

Huws left them at the garden gate. As he had a quick look around the outside and the stunning, he found himself thinking of ending his days in a remote cottage such as this. Elin grown up and in her own home, his mother likely- he didn't finish he thought. He knew Gwen would have loved this place too, messing in the garden, and knowing her, baking scones and making tea for coastal path walkers. He was day dreaming again. A luxury that he rarely allowed himself.

He put his head through the door, taking care not to actually step indoors without full forensic overalls on.

"How are you doing in here, anything useful for us yet?" He indicated with a wave for the SOCO officer to come to the door, if nothing else, just to negate the need to shout his answer, knowing the two outside would be hanging onto every word.

"Decent fingerprints all over basically, and we may well get some DNA off pillows as we have found a few hairs which we will presume as his. Most of these cottages are spotless for the next visitor, and we assume this would have had clean fresh bedding before we had to lock down, can you ask them?" he nodded his head in the direction of the owners.

"Was the cottage cleaned after the last guests?" asked Huws.

The wife looked a little embarrassed, "Well no, the last lockdown was announced on a Friday and we actually had to ask the last guests to just pack and leave. We have a lady who cleans for us locally but told her to leave it to air until we knew when we could welcome either our next guests or indeed come up here ourselves."

Huws passed on this information indoors. "Ok, well, that isn't a huge problem because we could eliminate guest hair if we can have contact details for them and maybe sent their local officers to do a sample swab for us."

"Fantastic, I will get them to send me the details of their last guests, I shouldn't think that would be a problem."

Conversations had, phone numbers exchanged, Huws was assured that this would be done promptly, though they would have to contact the local self-catering agency that dealt with their bookings.

Nothing more for him to do here for now, he left, hoping there may be some news awaiting him back at the station. He manouvered his car in the limited space on the lane, he doubted there had been this many parked cars here for a fair time. Thankfully it was a dead end, so no hassle with people needing to pass. They had also opened the field gate alongside the cottage so the bigger forensics vans could park out of the way.

He raised a hand to the cottage owners, thinking they were very likely going to have to drive all the way back from whence they came that evening with all hotels and B&Bs shut, he imagined they would not be best pleased.

He meandered his way along the lane, back to the main road, not being able to resist crawling along and peering over the hedgerows. He knew that the search locally had not found anything as yet. No way could he have totally disappeared. Time would tell. This guy may well be as elusive as their previous case's guilty party had proved to be, and indeed no doubt that was still out there somewhere.

Arriving at the incident room, he had barely removed his jacket when Rogers the disheveled, as he had labelled him that morning, raised his arm for attention whilst holding the phone to his ear. Huws waited for him to finish his conversation and stop writing down whatever he was being told.

"Sir, a possible development. A report has come in to the local office in Wallasey on the Wirral from a guy who says his RIB has been stolen sometime in the last five days from a local boatyard. He hasn't been using it regularly now due to lockdown. It's gone, trailer, cans of fuel, everything, so obviously towed away and possibly hidden or launched wherever they managed it. Likely at night. The boat description matches ours that was retrieved with the bodies, now tied to the pontoon in Menai Bridge. I'm just about to forward them a photo of the boat so we can have a definite identity for it. That might well point towards a drug run from Liverpool area. We need to ask the police in that area to check any cameras that may be at any likely launching sites. We also need to get them to check whether we have any towing vehicles and trailers left somewhere unusual. This now makes it a bloody national crime at this rate. A big job now Guv."

"Indeed, so we better get on with it. Can you concentrate on the Wallasey side then Rogers please?"

He turned his attention then to whether there had been any feedback from the News release of the photos. Not yet it seemed, but some news on Richard flint from Essex, the police had come up with a couple of his next of kin. Generally, they hadn't involved themselves with him if it could be helped. It seems he was not popular with his family either. He was known as a junkie, as his brother-in-law called him. His house in the village well known as a drug den. Seems they are quite pleased he is out of the equation. The landlord of his house is also pretty pleased to get rid of him. The car definitely belonged to him too.

The local teams down there are this very minute searching the house for any possible links or computer messages arranging some sort of deal. They reported the house being a total tip and generally a health hazard of filth, it could take a while. What they needed now was an ID on the boatmen and the runaway who was currently the biggest worry and risk to the general public.

Possibly, now it was getting to the time of day when people would be settling down to have their tea and watch a bit of TV, catching up on their social media and the early evening news, maybe if they were very lucky, it would provide some news by the morning that would help. He subconsciously crossed his fingers and toes in desperate hope.

Chapter Twenty-Three

HE STOOD UP AND STRETCHED, surprising himself on that he had actually slept for a full three hours. Catching up no doubt on missed sleep.

He needed to think strategically now, how best to get to Bangor and the station, a plan was forming, but it would be a risk. However, he had taken a few of those these last couple of days and so far, he was still free. Pointless maybe in reality, as now he had very little of the actual cash. As far as he was aware though they wouldn't have an ID for him or know who he was. He reckoned if he chose the right opportunity, he could possibly accomplish the next step easily.

He dusted himself off and set off down the track. He shortly arrived at a pair of huge rusting gates near a lodge house. Thankfully there seemed to be no one around and the gate was openable, albeit with some efforts accompanied by loud creaks and squeaks. It bought him down to a main road where there was no option other than to keep his head down and try his best to look casual. He might make it a little way along the road and get a bit further until he saw the right opportunity.

Cars passed, seemingly oblivious. That was one advantage of lockdown, it was unlikely that anyone would slow down and offer him a lift. He wondered in fact if he could make it from here to Bangor on foot, could he take the chance? In that split second, a garage door opened on his left side, a row of garages, clearly servicing the houses that hung on to the hillside to his left running steeply down to the sea. He hung back to allow the car to reverse across his path, smiling at its occupant, a sly smirk of satisfaction, this was meant to happen. Best laid plans and all that going out of the window. She noticed him, and smiled back, a smile which disappeared in an instance as he grabbed the door handle and opened it. He leapt into the seat as his left hand pulled the pistol from his belt. She saw it immediately and froze, her fingers rigid around the steering wheel.

"No one will get hurt if you just drive. Bangor station, quickest way. Get on with it, no playing silly buggers."

She took a big breath, and without a word, pulled onto the road and set off.

"Put your foot down a bit, I haven't got all day." She was a pretty woman, in different times he might well have fancied her, she looked to have taken care of herself. Clearly from her clothes and car, she was well heeled.

"It changes into a thirty area just around the corner, there's always a speed trap van in the layby over the bridge. I don't want another three points." She complained.

Jesus, he thought, she was talking as if she was going shopping with him, not being held at gunpoint. He sneered. The town of Menai Bridge seemed quiet, all the shops seemed to be shut, other than the chip shop he saw on his right. What wouldn't he give now for a chippy dinner? No time though.

She turned left onto the ornate bridge, straight onto the mainland it seemed, he relaxed a little as he imagined his destination looming nearer and nearer.

Suddenly the car stopped, he lurched forwards unrestrained onto the dashboard, she had caught him out, he had taken his eye off the ball and had looked at the sea passing under the bridge.

In a flash before he could react, she was out of the car, and moving behind the vehicle. To his absolute fury, he realised in an instance that he couldn't open the door, she had parked the car right up against the left side of the archway, she had also locked the door. Clever cow, he couldn't see her anywhere, she must be in the archway on the other carriageway. Sod it, he was fucking trapped.

She was shaking from head to foot, barely able to speak to the emergency operator, who assured her the police would be there in no time and to stay out of the line of fire. A car stopped in front of her, unable to cross the bridge, the driver jumped out, concerned as to her reasoning for being there, to say he was gobsmacked to hear that she had been held at gunpoint in her own car was an under-statement.

"I need to stop other cars getting onto the bridge," he said as he hopped back in and reversed as far as he could the way he had come, and immediately could be seen disappearing around the curve of the road to, she presumed stop any other cars. Unfortu-nately, by now there were three cars behind hers and a man with a gun sitting inside it. Not a lot she could do about that. She did however frantically indicate to them the need to keep their heads down. She just had to wait it out until the police came. She prayed to God they would not be long.

Chapter Twenty-Four

"I THINK we may have him Sir," shouted Rogers, Howard on his feet quick as a flash.

"Where is the bastard, I want a few words with him."

"Sit down, this is not something you want to get involved in at this stage." Huws was grabbing his jacket.

Rogers added that the ARV was on its way to the bridge with a firearms team on board. The local bobbies having been told to stand by on both sides of the bridges, some of our Anglesey lads and some Bangor officers. Huws put on his vest as did Rogers.

Rogers would drive him in one of the squad cars, Huws was never keen on being driven, particularly on blues. There were a few officers running from the Llangefni Station at that precise moment, making for various cars. They left the compound in a blue topped snaking line, sirening their way along to the roundabout and off for the A55, the quickest route to the incident. He feared there would be a bit of red mist amongst the drivers, anger already churning up at the chance of getting the man who killed young Parry.

Feeder roads onto the bridge on both sides had already been blocked off by traffic unit cars, an effort to keep members of the public away from the scene.

This would have to be approached with a structured plan of action, knowing he was still armed.

Huws got out of the car, walking towards the head of the armed task force team, he instructed her that he wanted the man taken alive if at all possible, a thought unspoken, Huws wanted him to rot in jail, not get out of this by being shot. Whether he shot himself or not, no one could predict. People like this were usually cowards to the core though. Time would tell.

The first on scene had now managed to get the cars which had entered the bridge to reverse to safety, though that had taken some time to guide a scared nonagenarian backwards, who may actually in truth not be that confident or competent going forwards.

The lady who had been carjacked was still in the archway next to the car, she was at least safe in there. The Bangor side of the bridge was also closed off, cars being diverted up the Treborth road towards the Britannia bridge an attempt at some semblance of normality.

Huws wondered if the bastard would recognize the voice coming at him through the loudhailer, it would have been the same that he had heard the night before the absolute tragedy.

"Get yourself over to the driver's side. We will open the door. Have the gun in your right hand, where we can see it, barrel towards yourself, both hands above your head and slowly get out of the car."

Nothing happened, Huws, registering that the scumbag didn't even turn his head, no doubt even now still thinking he might somehow get away with it. The order was repeated, more menace this time, everyone, he knew damn well would be wanting to see this monster put behind bars.

The first of the firearms teams from both ends started the approach, walking on the pedestrian pathway behind the chain structure, knowing, that if he tried to get a shot that it may well protect them a fair bit. The lads coming from Menai Bridge behind the car were likely a little safer. The lady from the car could now be seen sensibly sitting down on the wall arch nearest the middle of the road. In Huws' opinion, she had been incredibly brave and exceptionally quick-thinking.

He was confident that this would end well. The bloke didn't really have much choice, although he was taking his time contemplating his options.

The loudhailer repeated the order. Obviously, it could not be assumed at this point that he only had the one form of firearm. Clearly, he had come here with the intention of committing his crime, but it was unlikely he would have carried anything with him on foot.

An almost tangible hush fell, if it was possible for it to be quieter. The gulls wheeling overhead had ceased their raucous squawking whilst the scene played out below them, even the speedboats taking tourists on fast boat rides up and down the Strait had been commanded to stop and stand- off, although the Beaumaris lifeboat had been asked to stand by directly below the bridge incase of any untoward stupidity by their man in a ludicrous effort to escape capture.

"Do you have any more weapons inside the car?" came the next request. The man could be seen shaking his head to the negative. Some response at last.

"Now slide across to the driver's seat and exit the door, which will be opened for you," a repeat of the same words that were minutes before ignored.

The nearest firearms officer indicated to the lady that she should use the key fob to open the door. This she duly did. The man was manouvering himself like a clumsy grizzly bear across the front seats of the car, trying to get his legs over the centre console. Four guns were aimed at him, he struggled to squeeze himself through the gap between the door and the car, a gap also restricted due to the confines of the archway.

Luckily the lady had been nimble and slight.

The pistol was held above his head by the barrel. Huws thought again that the woman deserved a medal for her quick thinking, though it had been a huge risk.

"Come forwards and get behind the car, hands in view,

turning away from us." A single armed officer, gun still very much poised to fire, moved forwards followed closely by a second officer who stepped forwards. One shouted the order for the gun to be placed on the floor which he did. The other officer then pulled both the man's arms behind his back and in a very practiced movement had him cuffed within seconds, despite the restricted space.

Pulling him away from the narrow gap they roughly checked him over for any more weapons, whilst repeatedly asking him if he was still armed. No response could be seen or heard, just an arrogant sneer on his face.

Another officer, knowing it was now safe was indicating that the woman should walk out of the archway and come to him through the bars of the bridge onto the pavement.

Huws made his way from the end of the bridge towards her. A traffic car making its way onto the bridge in readiness to take away the prisoner. A couple of SOCO team members were also already booted and suited to check the car, though Huws reckoned they would do better to get the car on a low loader to take it away in an effort to get the traffic moving again. His suggestion was agreed on. As he got closer to the lady who was now chatting away with the officer, Huws recognized her, astounded, Jane!

"Sir, this is Miss Jane Mathews. He jumped in her car outside her garage on the Glyn Garth Road."

"Thank you, officer, we have already been introduced, and in fact this lady does an awful lot of work on our behalf at our local autopsy suite, and very skilled she is too, and obviously has a secret criminal catching string to her bow as well."

"Funny old world we now live in, I never expected an adventure like this, this afternoon, you certainly owe me a fish and chip dinner for this Idris." She smiled, the officer passing her a mask out of his pocket. Dispensing of its cellophane wrapper in her pocket she put in on.

"I truly hate these things. I've used them at work daily for years but to have to use them everywhere else, really gets me, but needs must I suppose, the sooner we get rid of this virus the better."

Huws was impressed that she could even appear this calm and logical after what she had been through.

As she was speaking, they could see the officer placing a mask onto the handcuffed detainee. He was put in the back of the traffic car with a little more care maybe than Huws would have afforded him. In fact, at this moment in time Huws wanted to defy all the rules in the books and go and give him a damn good hammering. Just the smirk as he was about to get into the car, that smirk. How he would have loved to have wiped that off his face.

Jane was now led away into another car, a little aggrieved that her trip out for her click and collect groceries had been thwarted, but she needed to give her statement, and her car was about to be towed away. Huws assured her, he would see her very shortly at the station, and would make sure her car was returned to her as quickly as possible. He left to follow the squad car to the station. His stomach was churning slightly at the thought of facing their man across a table.

Chapter Twenty-Five

THIS WOULD BE no simple custody suite job; a huge forensics involvement would be essential. Their first hurdle had been the absolute refusal of the accused to even divulge his name. Not even a no comment, just absolute dumb silence. He was stripped down to his underpants, searched, fingerprinted, mouth swabbed, all procedures which had to be carried out to the letter of the law. A grey track suit roughly pushed towards him.

There was a background hum of voices from the office space behind the Perspex sheeting, clearly a result of officers knowing full well who was about to be led down the corridor to his cell, all wanting a look at him to be able to put a face to their venom. It would be so hard to maintain a professional distance with this man.

It was going to be a challenge pinning all the murders on him. Maybe he was only responsible for Parry's death. Time and evidence gathering would definitely be proof of that. Thankfully plenty of fingerprints and DNA evidence had been found at the cottage and likely in the car, to link him with at least PC Parry's murder. This made it more likely they would be given the time to pin the others on him as was suspected. At the moment they had absolutely no evidence at all as to who he actually was. He had however nodded his head when he was asked if he wanted a lawyer present at the interview.

Huws would be very careful in choosing his questions. He would leave him in the cell to stew for a while, pretty certain they could nail the murder of Parry on him once they had the forensics back. That meant he would be charged, after all Justin Howard had been asked to identify him as soon as he was bought in and he confirmed it was the same man.

Tomorrow he would be taken to court, and due to evidential proof, would be detained for further questions.

Idris Huws went through to the staff kitchen and turned on the kettle. A coffee was needed before he faced him, not really feeling yet that the job was a success, but first of all needing a chat with Jane who was currently in another office down the corridor giving her statement. She would appreciate a cuppa and he wanted to personally check up on her.

He tidied up his collar and ran his hands through his hair, seriously needing a haircut and a shave, she would unlikely be impressed. Covid barber shop closures having a lot to answer for. Before he could make his way down the corridor, cups in hand, Rogers stepped in through the door,

"We have some CCTV footage of two lads launching a RIB off the slipway onto New Brighton beach and leaving the vehicle there, much to the consternation of the public, the plates on the four by four are off a stolen vehicle found dumped not far from John Moore's main university building. We're just waiting for CCTV from the Kingsway tunnel onto the M53 which is the way they likely went. This is well planned and unless we get an ID on the guys this is going to take time.

We're planning on releasing the boat tomorrow; forensics have got everything they can off it and the bloke who owns it will meet one of our officers down by the pier in Menai Bridge early afternoon. He's already picked up his trailer in New Brighton, the lads over that end have got any prints they could off it. We're taking in the four by four, it may well also be stolen but we will check vin numbers to see if we can trace an owner. It could, if luck is on our side, belong to one of the men."

"Good work." Huws was always pleased to know that his teams were busy following all avenues in the background. This was their biggest job for a long long time, and things were going like clock-work, loose ends coming together nicely. He suspected that the murder of PC Steffan Parry was playing a big part in the urgency and interest in this investigation too.

Jane was waiting for him in the reception area, statement given.

"Well Jane Mathews, turns out that not only are you an exem-plary autopsy room assistant you are also a bit of a hero. I doubt we would have caught him if he had maybe picked on someone else. He may have made it onto a train and disappeared back into the seedy world of drug crime, never to be seen again."

"Well, if truth be known, as I was giving my statement, the reality and sheer stupidity of what I did hit me. I should have just dropped him at Bangor Station and that would be the end of my involvement, but I guessed straight away that this was the man who had shot Steffan Parry, and It was like a fury was released inside me. I was going to get him whatever it took.

I only decided what to do when I saw an Arriva bus slow right down to get through the first arch, wing mirror on the driver's side pulled in.

I knew the gun was in his belt on his left, so I chanced driving as close as I could to the left wall, just giving me enough space to jump out, it was just lucky really that he hadn't given me a chance to put my seat belt on when he jumped in, I would normally have got out to shut the garage door. My car has a keyless ignition and the key was actually in my pocket, so I pushed the off button and leapt out, pushing the key fob to lock as soon as I had slammed the door. I just went around the corner into the other arch then to get away. I was worried though because three other cars pulled up right behind mine, I was so afraid of other people being caught in the crossfire. Poor Steffan, I can't believe that he got caught in the middle of this."

"You did really well, unbeknown to us then, the gun was empty, so other people were as safe as we could be sure of. Now can I give you a lift home?" asked Huws.

"I'd rather you gave me a lift to Morrisons, Bangor first to pick up my shopping, or else I'll starve," she said with a wink.

"Of course, I will, no problem. We're not ready to interview this guy anyway until we have a couple more forensic links in the chain back, it will also give me a bit of breathing space to calm down, before I speak to the scumbag... sorry , that was unprofessional of me," apologised Huws.

"Idris, we are all human, it is totally normal to feel like this after what has happened." She placed a comforting hand on his arm. It made him feel good that she also used his first name. He was always Sir, or DI these days to everyone other than his mother.

Not having much of a life outside work meant there were no friends since Gwen had gone. Most of 'their' friends had, it proved actually been 'hers', and in the main melted away after her death, though he was fully aware that his lack of openness and approacha-bility after Gwen's sudden departure played a huge part in their disappearance.

Jane followed him to the car, Huws holding the passenger door open for her,

"Well thank you kind Sir, it's a long time since anyone has held a car door, or any door in fact, for me."

He smiled, "Probably too many women around now that make us feel as if we are being hugely sexist doing such things. We can't seem to do right for wrong these days." Idris Huws smiled as he shut the door.

Chapter Twenty-Six

SHOPPING DULY PICKED UP; Huws drove Jane home. He had found her easy to talk to, conversation flowing, occasional laughter, in a way that he had not been able to chat since Gwen had died.

Obviously, most of the conversation was about work, but no pregnant pauses or silences, it lifted his mood more than he could have imagined in a short twenty-minute run from shop to home.

"I would invite you in for coffee," said Jane. "With all these Covid guidelines, it will have to wait, and the apartment could do with a serious tidy. I've been terribly lazy with my housework since we are not allowed visitors, any excuse." she laughed. Don't forget though you owe me a chip shop dinner when it is allowed."

"I think you deserve a slightly better meal than a chippy dinner for all your effort today, I won't forget."

Huws left her, feeling as if a ton weight had been lifted off his head, somehow putting a spring in his step, even though he was sat driving the car. He smiled to himself at this daft thought, turned the radio on and hummed along to Que sera sera as he made his way back through Menai Bridge and on to Llangefni.

He wondered if there had been any further developments since he had left. He chuckled to himself at the thought that the team wouldn't need to know that he had driven a witness to Morrisons to get their shopping. Tapping his fingers along to the tune on the shiny worn leathered steering wheel. Some of his cheeriness dissipating as he remembered how Parry had enjoyed his short drive of his 'antique' car.

Meanwhile at the station, Howard was still head down in his laptop, resolutely working on any tiny fact that he could find. He had barely uttered an exchange of words with his colleagues, he felt brittle, unable to speak for fear of breaking down, knowing in all honesty that he wasn't fit to work but what else could he do? He hated the thought of being in their home alone with his thoughts. He saw Huws coming in through the door, maybe he had more news- turns out he didn't.

"Right, do we have the information we need at hand now to pin this on our accused? We know that he is at this very moment in the top interview room talking to the duty lawyer. Once that's finished, we can interview him. Rogers are you happy to sit in with me. Can you make sure we have everything we need?"

"Yes Sir, we now have definite fingerprint and numerous DNA links to put him at the murder scene prior to Parry's shooting." She glanced across at Howard before continuing. "The man in custody has been positively identified by DS Howard, to be the same man that he saw exiting the house and shooting Steff. Uhm, PC Steffan Parry," her voice cracked a tad at this disclosure, looking again at Howard, who had his head down.

"We have fingerprints from the car that was parked at the crime scene, both on the steering, door handle and the bag of money and likewise the drugs. We also have other prints from the car that we assume are Richard Flint's, we are just waiting for any records to confirm Flints prints from a previous drink driving offence a couple of years ago committed in Essex. That will give a definite link between the two men.

What we can't do however is prove as yet that this man killed Flint. I say this man, because he still as yet refuses to give us his name. We are also struggling at the moment to prove that he could have shot the two men in the boat."

"Today," cut in Huws, "we will concentrate on getting some justice for Parry. Get the man to court and charged before the end of the day, that will give us time to further question him. He'll go to trial for the murder of Parry, but it would be good to be able to tie up any loose ends. Thank you, Rogers, I will join you in the corridor in a minute, I just need a word with someone first.".

Huws asked Howard to join him in his own office.

"Right, young man, sit down here and talk to me, I really don't think you should be here today. Why don't you go home and get your head down? You look like shit?"

Howard looked down at his hands, fingers tightly clenched together until the knuckles were white. "I'm fine Sir, I am happier here with something to focus on than at home alone with my thoughts. I don't know how I will cope now though, the funeral and stuff, I'm going to have to take a total back seat. Steffan, had never told his mum and dad, that he was gay, his dad was very old fash-ioned you know, and Steffan was convinced he would have disowned him or something like that, despite me begging him to be open. They used to visit us only very occasionally at home, but if we knew they were coming, I would disappear for a few hours, or even arrange it so I was at work. It was hard because we couldn't really have any evidence of us being together in the house. They were always telling him he needed to find a nice girlfriend to share the nice house with him, and all that sort of stuff. I feel as if all our life and history together is all of a sudden gone, he will be buried as 'the dearly loved son of...' No mention of me and how much we loved each other. We had plans you know, we were going to do our thirty years in the force, and build up our savings, then enjoy our combined pensions. We had a secret competition as to how high we could get promoted before retirement.

We loved Norway and planned to buy a coastal property there on the Lofoten islands that we both fell in love with on a holiday, run a holiday business from there, taking tourists paddle boarding and kayaking and having people stay to see the Northern lights.

It's all gone now. I loved him so much."

Huws was a little lost for words, he had never been much of an agony aunt but one thing he did understand was just how lost young Justin Howard was at this point in time.

Justin continued amongst stifled sobs, trying desperately to speak without actually howling. His eyes were full of un-spilled tears.

"There is no way I can tell his parent's all this now is there; it might totally taint their view of their son. But you know, it shouldn't change things, he was the most loving, caring kind generous man you would meet, so clever and obsessive about getting on at work. He was so proud when I got promoted to DS straight from a constable, but he told me then whilst laughing about it that I had a competition on my hands. He wanted to beat me into your shoes when you retired, I'm absolutely sure he would have done it."

Justin seemed small and exhausted in the chair. Clasped hands bloodless still with the desperation of their clenching.

Huws had no suitable words to offer, but understood, how being at work would be better any day than being home alone. He had been guilty of doing the same himself to an extent, and in fact he still did. Poor Howard had a very long road ahead of him in his grief and loss.

"Only, you can decide, how best to move forwards from here, but if you want in any way to help them keep Steffan's memory alive for the three of you, it may be good for them to know exactly what you are telling me now. That ok, he did live a bit of a double life where they were concerned, and even here at work where you kept it quiet and on a professional footing, but maybe, once it is out in the open, they will appreciate that he was very much loved and cared for. Maybe his old dad will be shocked initially, and that is something you may have to face, but give them time to absorb it, you never know, you may all feel better for it. It is a decision only you can make.

Now, go make yourself a coffee and wash your face, take one of the lads with you down to Prince's pier to meet the owner of the boat. Have a chat with him, get his contact details and just suss the waters a little, just in case there is an off chance that he was in fact involved with the plan in any way, shape or form."

Huws knew as Justin left the office that hopefully he may be able to see some light at the end of a currently very dark tunnel and understand that his colleagues would go out of their way to support him in any-way they could.

Huws recognized that he could not put off any longer his need to sit face to face across the table with their man. He was hoping to God, he didn't smirk or sneer, or he would be sorely tempted to smash his face up.

Chapter Twenty-Seven

ROGERS AND HUWS sat down opposite a slouching sloth of a man, his lawyer sitting next to him, all lipstick and big hair. She didn't offer a smile.

"My client has agreed to tell you his name and address but has chosen thereafter to not comment until definite and substantial proof of indisputable evidence is presented to us."

Huws took a breath to calm himself before stating that it was his right to do so but that she ought to know perfectly well, that a name and address and date of birth was actually required by the law. He had no choice. He was told by Rogers that the interview would be recorded both by tape recorder and via video. He read him his rights, regarding the fact that he had been arrested and charged on a suspicion of murder, that he had a right to contact a friend or relative to let them know where he was, as well as any medical treatment which may be necessary anytime through the proceedings. He also, at this moment had the right to not have his details exposed to the media. There was no response from him other than he shuffled in his chair, sat back overconfidently, and folded his arms. He also smirked. Huws took a big breath and whistled the air out through clenched teeth, jaw set as if to block the exit of a fury that once released could not be contained.

Rogers asked for his name, he looked across at his lawyer who nodded in the affirmative.

"Robert Littleton, born June 24th, 1970."

"Address?" added Rogers. "Haven't got one, wife kicked me out, been dossing in friend's houses since then," he grunted as if expecting some sympathy.

"What was your address then, when you did live at home?" Rogers persevered.

"22 Oak Tree Mews, Middleton near Chelmsford, Essex."

"What was your connection with Richard Flint, the man who is the registered owner of the car that was found at the cottage where the murder of PC Steffan Parry took place?" Huws knew that the interview was going to be frustratingly and infuriatingly tedious from now on. No answer, not even a 'No comment'.

"My client will not offer any more information until we have some evidence on the table, it is for you to prove my client's guilt not for us to deny at this stage."

Huws was so tempted at this point to throttle the information out of the guy sat opposite him, a fury that he didn't even recognize as his own was dangerously close to erupting. He fought hard to contain his temper.

Huws tried a different tack, "You called for help via 999 on the night of the 18th of August at 10.30 pm, the Coastguard service were called out and attended to you, assisting you to the top of the cliff. You had, you claimed, hurt your leg. One team member dealt with an injury on your face that you claimed you had sustained in a short fall whilst fishing. We have a transcript of that call to play you."

Rogers pushed the button on a laptop, the hoarse breathless voice of Robert Littleton demanding an ambulance due to him having hurt his leg and being at the bottom of a steep slope.

"The ambulance crew turned up on scene and after they checked your leg over, you became quite obstructive and refused further treatment and walked off, very likely you just wanted help to get up the steep slope."

Littleton simply shrugged his shoulders. "You said, you had been fishing, but no evidence of fishing paraphernalia was found when the coastguards checked later, just a few empty beer cans and food wrappers which they cleared away. Why was this? What did you do with the fishing gear? That statement in itself slaps a Covid travel breach on you, but it's the least of your problems at the moment I should imagine, so, tell us, where is your rod and other accoutrements?"

Another shrug. This was not going to get them very far, thought Huws.

"Was Richard Flint down on the shore there with you? Did you argue and then take his car? Did you kill Roger Flint?" continued Huws.

The lady across the table piped up at this point. "And this has what exactly to do with my client being arrested for the murder of a police officer?"

She had a point, but neither Huws nor Rogers wanted to concede. However, they had to stick to the rules.

"Why was a car registered to another dead man, Roger Flint hidden behind the house that you, on evidence of fingerprints broke into at Caim near Penmon. Your fingerprints were discovered in the car as well as on a large quantity of heroin and a wad of cash hidden under the spare tyre?" He surprised them both by offering an answer.

"No idea, it isn't my car, nothing to do with me, I don't even know a Richard Flint".

"How do you explain the prints then?" asked Rogers. No answer this time.

Huws knew that if they could pin enough evidence on this guy, they could buy themselves time to work further on the other deaths which he was convinced were down to him too, or even down to both Flint and Littleton.

"We have CCTV footage of you both at the general store in Llangoed earlier in the day of your fishing' incident."

Rogers again pushed the laptop in his direction enabling a view of the screen.

"Do you agree that this is you and a second individual that we have identified as a Richard Flint? Did you just by chance drive together to the area, a rough journey give or take a few miles, of three hundred miles, then stop in the same shop and then drive away in the direction that could have taken you to White Beach, it sounds preplanned to me. Did you forget to pack your fishing rods? Did you have an argument?"

Lady lawyer saw fit to butt in again at this point.

"I need to remind you that my client has not at this point been arrested in a case involving a Richard Flint. Can you stick to the subject matter please?"

Huws barely paused in his questioning, "We have put you at the cottage in Caim, again we have fingerprint evidence and DNA evidence from hairs on the pillow to glassware and crockery. We also have a positive ID of you leaving the cottage by the back-bedroom window and shooting our young Police officer PC Steffan Parry. A young man with his whole life ahead of him, and you did not even pause for a second before pulling the trigger and making off. This makes us also suspect that not only are you responsible for the death of PC Parry but that you or Flint between you are responsible for the deaths of the two men who were in the boat. And you may well be responsible for the death of Flint. What do you have to say to that?"

Both Huws and Rogers knew that as yet they had no evidence whatsoever to prove that the two men had been shot by Littleton or Flint, they were after all a few miles at sea when they were found, but things like this didn't happen every day around here, there had to be a link.

"Nothing to do with me," he said with that same self- righteous spiteful look. "Prove it."

Huws looked across at Rogers and realised that today at least, there would be absolutely no point whatsoever in continuing any further on the matter of the other deaths, but Huws stood up and looked down at the disheveled scruff bag who was sitting on the chair as if he was casually watching tv.

"Robert Littleton I am arresting you on the suspicion of murdering Police Constable Steffan Parry on the 21st of August 2020. You do not have to say anything, but it may harm your-"

" Yeh, yeh, yeh, I know all that crap," butted in Littleton.

Huws continued. "Harm your defense if you do not mention when questioned something you later rely on in court. Anything you do say, may be given in evidence." Huws shut the file in front of him with a ferocity that Rogers had not seen previously in a man who always appeared to be calm and quiet.

She opened the interview room door and nodded at two uniformed officers to take him to the cells. Clearly Huws was incapable temporarily of speech. "He will be appearing in court later this afternoon."

Lady lawyer as Huws regarded her, stood up and straightened her short skirt over her knees.

"We will be seeing each other again very soon, no doubt about it," she said on leaving the room, clacketing along the corridor in her blood red high heeled shoes, designer no doubt.

It still defeated Idris Huws that these defense lawyers could in fact actually defend scum like Littleton and his ilk, knowing full well that they were guilty. The whole team needed to pull their finger out now to build up this case around him, and weave in as best they could evidence for the other one, or maybe even the three deaths.

Chapter Twenty-Eight

HUWS FELT EXHAUSTED. He should have been pleased to have got their man, but he realised he'd not had a square meal since God knows when, or a proper night's sleep come to that. He would go home this evening. As far as he was aware there was nothing he was needed for or that the team couldn't deal with themselves until morning. He did however call his DS and ask if all had gone well at the pier. It seemed it had, with no reason to suspect the boat owner of involvement, but that he did have all his details if by any chance they needed him in the future. Idris instructed him to go home and put his head down. Howard was reluctant, Huws understood the ghosts he feared were waiting for him at home, in the form of silence and memories which would hit him with the same jack boot in the gut force, as if he had been actually physically struck. Huws knew it would be no different if he did not go home tonight or any night that week, it would still be waiting for him. He felt for him. He hurt for him.

The journey home passed in a bit of a blur, thoughts regarding the case playing in front of him like a cinematic display. He pulled into a farm track entrance between Talwrn and Pentraeth and switched the engine off. He got out and locked the car. Walking back along the road the way he came, he entered a footpath opposite the popular Stone Science Museum, he chose to walk down it's rough track, clearly once a drove road or similar, muddied and poached by numerous cattle. He needed to breathe the non- polluted Anglesey air, not the sweaty stale fug of the incident room. Fresh air, or the strong smell of cattle at least, may clear his head and help him organise his thoughts.

This is something he had done in the immediate aftermath of losing Gwen. He had often walked in the dead of night, alone with just his thoughts for company. Occasionally he would clip a half asleep, surprised Ben onto his extending lead, following his master unenthusiastically having been awoken from his old dog slumbers. Elin however had chosen to go back to school straight after the funeral. Claiming that the company of her friends would be better for her. He was not in the right head space to either agree or resist, so she had gone her own way.

Head down, he continued along the path, not actually taking in the surrounding greenness and sweet aroma of a very late cut crop of hay. Thankfully, it slightly masked the aroma of cowpat as he progressed up the hill. Gwen always claimed it was a healthy albeit unhealthy smell.

Climbing slightly now up the other side of the valley, he puffed and blew. He needed to work on his growing paunch. Gwen would have nagged him.

He shook his head in disbelief that she had been taken first, after all the care she took with her diet.

When he hit the country lane at the path end, instead of retracing his steps to the start, he decided to turn left and continue along the back lane towards the tiny rural village of Talwrn, still very much daylight, it would kill time before he would have to face the questioning tongue of his mother.

How he wished that he could have a bit of space, just him and Elin, for a while. To go home, sit in his own chair, watch 'The Chase' as he and Gwen did when they could. Sit with his thoughts and memories. His old mum seemed to believe for some reason- upbringing maybe, that to grieve was a sign of lack of resilience, that life must move on. She had, he supposed at her age, lost far more people than he had. It may indeed be the acceptance that comes with age.

He did appreciate however, that he would be returning to a tidy house, all but Elin's bedroom cleaned and cleaned again. His mother was on a warning to never enter Elin's teenage domain. His clothes would have been washed and ironed and no doubt there would be a meal waiting for him to be warmed or God forbid a healthy salad. His mother's salads were no comparison to Gwen's. He smiled to himself, Gwen's salads were a relatively filling meal of a huge variety of fresh ingredients, his mothers were inevitably two leaves of lettuce, a few slices of cucumber, half a tomato, a rolled-up slice of ham which his mother believed was 'posh', maybe a pickled onion, and a hard- boiled egg cut in half. Hardly satiating a hungry appetite. Her salads had certainly not evolved with modern times.

He strolled, hands in pocket, back towards the centre of Talwrn, the scent of early wheat harvests filling the air, the crops now matured and ready for combining. These narrow roads during late summer, were often full to bursting with huge modern tractors and trailers with fat wheels which cut into verges and bank edges permanently destroying them. The Red campion and Primroses that appeared religiously in early spring, long disappeared now from the cut verges. The country lanes of Anglesey had always been better suited to horse and cart.

He was quite shocked when he realised he was whistling. The purposeful pacing was clearly doing some good. He turned left at the crossroads and made for the last stretch back to the car, not quite so pleasant this bit being a main road. If some of the drivers hurtling past him knew they were passing an officer of the law at such speeds they would be horrified, mind you, maybe the speed trap van would be down in the dip in Pentraeth, that was quite a good spot to catch them. He smiled again, thinking he had better have his wits about him and remember to watch his own speed entering the village. Coming down the hill and suddenly hitting the thirties caught out everyone other than the wisest. There was nothing for it now other than to meander back home.

He had barely driven two miles out of Pentraeth when his phone rang. He cursed the lack of a Bluetooth facility in his car, though he doubted he would understand it anyway. Pulling up by a redundant telephone exchange box and answered. It was Rogers.

"We have a possible ID on the two men in the boat. Two ne'er do wells from the Wrexham area, one from Coed Poeth the other from Ruabon. A local man has phoned up saying that he had seen the photos on our Facebook page, then again on the local news. He has a name for both of them, Patrick Flint and Kyle Williams."

"Patrick Flint?"

"Yes Sir, we are assuming at this point that he may well be related to Richard Flint in some way, age wise, either a son or a nephew, but Colchester police are already onto that now. We're just waiting for this fella to tell us which is which."

"Good. Good work, well, not a lot you need me for tonight. I'll just touch base with Justin this evening, so unless something pressing happens, I'll see you bright and early tomorrow." Huws felt hopeful that maybe, just maybe the story was just coming together.

He stepped indoors. "I'm just taking Ben for a short walk, your supper is in the fridge," announced his mother, pausing in the hallways with the lead in her hand. Huws knew she was besides herself with the desperation to ask questions but understanding by now that no answers would be forthcoming, she left the house. He smiled when he heard her muttering under her breath, that no one ever told her anything.

His salad was in the fridge. No ham, half a pork pie today, more jelly than meat which he had always hated, and a side of crisps. He shook his head and enjoyed the peace and quiet of a half hour by himself in his own kitchen. He loved her really, but bloody hell it was hard work reverting back to his ten-year-old self, every time he entered his own front door.

Supper eaten, no doubt to be followed by some biscuits later, he was still hungry. Always his downfall according to Gwen.

Dialing Justin's mobile number, it went straight to voicemail.

Huws was in a quandary now, worrying as to his state of mind. He left a message asking how he was. What a stupid question he thought, as soon as the words came out of his mouth. People had been asking him that for months after Gwen died, he had been tempted on many occasions to say he actually felt like shit, but people don't really want to hear that, they ask often out of politeness, not to get ensnared into a ' woe is me' conversation. People often avoided him in order to not to have to ask him at all.

"I'm hoping you've had some food and you're having an early night, see you in the morning if you are up to coming to the station. We have some ID on the boatmen which is quite interesting. Another piece of a jigsaw it seems." He hung up, part of him wanting to go over to Justin's house to check on him, but he was after all a grown man. He would see him tomorrow.

Chapter Twenty-Nine

HUWS ARRIVED at the incident room to find it bustling, a hive of activity, you could smell the excitement in the room, or maybe that was just yesterday's stale sweat.

"Christ you lot, you might well be busy, but come on let's have a tidy up in here, if you don't empty these paper baskets we will have Rats and mice and god knows what other vermin nesting in them, throw a couple of those windows open and get some fresh air in here."

He was pleased to see that DS Justin Howard was at his desk. He feared that Howard would do exactly as he had done himself, burying his brain in his work and not allow the feelings of loss to overcome him. They had the funeral to get through first. He had promised Steffan's parents that there would be police representation at the funeral. Whether Howard would be amongst them time would tell.

"Ok, do we have anything back from Colchester yet?"

"Not yet Sir," answered young Richards who had been with him to see Steffan's parents.

"They're going to knock a few doors in Colne Engaine, however you pronounce the name, and see if anyone recognizes this Flint guy as a son or relative or maybe even a younger brother of Richard Flint, though they aren't holding out much hope. It's a nice quiet village, and I think as Flint was seen as a bit of a dodgy character, no one did anything with him, but we may get lucky, apparently, he did visit the Three Bells, the local pub. They'll ask in there too. It may take a couple of days. Littleton was remanded into custody yesterday pending trial. No doubt he's now concocting his story with his lawyer. It gives us a bit of breathing space to build up the file against him and see what we can get with the other three."

Huws could barely believe that they had in the space of a few days got four murders in this beautiful corner of Anglesey. He needed to get to grips with this and quickly.

"Sir," it was Howard, holding the phone towards him and covering the mouthpiece.

"It's Holyhead Coastguard Ops room, apparently there is a report of what appears to be a body washed up on the Sound side of Ynys Seiriol, that is Puffin Island Sir".

"Christ. Yes, I know where it is."

Huws moved across to take the call. He grabbed a pen off Howard's desk and scribbled on a pad. "Right, the Coastguard team are on scene, and have confirmed on observation with binoculars that the object that the first informant, a member of the public who was parked there in his motorhome, has seen could well be a body. Holyhead, on this confirmation have just authorized the lifeboat to launch. Again. This is pretty unbelievable now. It's becoming more like the last case by the day.

Rogers and Richards, if you can get down to Penmon point pronto just to keep an eye on the proceedings, maybe communicate via the Coastguard radios with the lifeboat crew. The team members will help you. God knows they have enough experience now.

It's may well be likely we will need to get ourselves and forensics onto the island, Howard and I will go straight to the lifeboat station." He nodded in Howards direction, "Are you happy to come? Can one of you here, just contact SOCO to meet me in Beaumaris at the boathouse and also contact the undertaker to meet us there, again." He repeated.

Lots of shuffling of papers, and scraping of chairs followed, as the chosen few made their way out. It was always good when you worked on a big job to have a new angle to follow.

Down on the point at Penmon four of the Coastguard team were already turning back cars and inquisitive walkers. Another team member was putting up blue striped tape at the entrance of the historical dovecote to prevent any more members of the public making their way down there.

The object could be seen on the beach opposite with the naked eye. Quite clear, even from across the swift moving sound that it was a clothed human body. The receding tide having left it high and dry for any vigilant person to see. Obviously, they couldn't get to it, but they could keep an eye on the proceedings.

They knew the lifeboat had launched. Aled, the Coastguard Station Officer, was on his way with Michael another experienced team member, to Beaumaris to receive the lifeboat when it eventually arrived back. Within fifteen minutes they could hear the thrumming of the two powerful outboards, the powerful orange inflatable appeared, bow up, cutting through the calm sea like slicing a cake. Very likely crewed by the same team that had been out the other day. The tide was currently ebbing so an approach on the eastern side of the small gravelled beach was only just possible, two crew members jumping into the shallows and making their way to the object on the beach. They took a look and with a wave of the arm they indicated that it was a body. They returned to their boat where radio comms to Holyhead were heard on the Penmon shore confirming that it was indeed a body. A male.

They were asked by the Ops room whether they would manage to bag the body between the crew, or did they require assistance. The police had already notified them that they would not require forensics to go onto the island. That made life a little easier for all concerned.

The crew could be observed laying the body onto the bag and

zipping it up. With a struggle they then carried it carefully towards the boat, feet slipping and sliding in the RNLI dry suit's inbuilt wellingtons.

Both Richards and Rogers thanked the Coastguard team members for their time and departed back towards Beaumaris. Hues had dealt more with the local teams in the last two or three years that he had throughout his police career.

DI Huws and DS Howard were waiting on the beach front for the arrival of the boat, two other Coastguard officers had now positioned themselves in order to try and reduce the likelihood of members of the public approaching the concrete apron in front of the open doors of the station. The tractor and trailer had already been driven into the water to receive the boat on her return.

Huws's mobile rang. He looked at the screen DCI Williams, his direct boss.

"Gov, what can I do for you?" asked Huws. The boss had generally let Huws get on with his cases without putting his nose in. He was based in Bangor, just across the Strait really from where they were now, however unlike himself, DCI Williams preferred office life, overseeing his men from behind his desk. Not one for traipsing around on the area's cliffs and beaches it seemed, unless he had to. Happy to trust Huws, although that case a couple of years back involving the cat, had caused some consternation.

"It seems you are being kept on your toes again with this case, four deaths in almost as many days." "Five possibly," butted in Huws.

"We're just on the foreshore in town awaiting the return of the lifeboat with a body washed up on the beach to the landward side of Ynys Seiriol, that is, Puffin Island. Of course, it may have no connection whatsoever with the other men, but we can't rule it out at this point."

"Oh, right, I hadn't caught up with this one."

"No Sir, it literally got reported to us by a member of the public with an astute eye near the lighthouse at Penmon Point. The body will be with us very shortly, I do have to admit to having a suspicion it may well be connected to the other deaths, or at least the two bodies in the RIB."

"RIB?" asked Williams.

"Rigid Inflatable boat Sir, like a rubber dinghy but with a more solid hull." That was Williams marine crafts lesson delivered by Huws who had himself only learnt the term when he had his return trip to Beaumaris from White beach only a few days ago. "Right, Idris, well keep me in the loop."

With a guffaw he added. "I hope to God these don't end up having been killed by a Panther, we'd be a laughing stock."

He hung up. Huws remembered the disbelief and ridicule he had suffered, the wrath of the DCI when he had first been told of the sighting of the big cat two years before. He knew it was possibly still out there, but he smiled to himself when the thought crossed his mind that as far as he was aware Panthers did not shoot guns.

When he turned back towards the boat, it was already sitting high and dry, secured in the trailer, being pulled up out of the water, hose reels at the ready, the shore crew preparing to wash off the corrosive saltwater. A few extra crew members at the ready to assist with the handling of the body onto the ground. Good timing too as the SOCO van turned up. These volunteers were worth their weight in gold thought Huws. Always ready to assist in times of trouble, along with the local coastguard teams, whom he had built a deep respect for.

The forensics team, obvious by their attire, cameras in hand, asked for the opening of the body bag. Huws and Howard watched the proceedings from a few feet away. There was already significant destruction to the facial features. The sea and its creatures already doing their damage, but the features could still be recognized as a male.

"Any idea on rough age?" asked Howard.

"Difficult to be precise on first look, but probably thirties. There's nothing to be gleaned from examining him further here at the moment. We'll get him to the mortuary and liaise with you from there. People are starting to gather, and I see that the undertaker has arrived".

Yet another body was carried onto a silver legged gurney and rolled along the concrete with as much dignity as possible and slid between the open doors of the black transit van for its short journey to the autopsy suite in Bangor. Rowlands would wonder what on earth was going on in the area. Certainly, it would keep him on his toes.

Chapter Thirty

HUWS THANKED the lifeboat crew and the Coastguard officers, adding that he hoped it would be a long time before her saw them again as it was becoming a bit of a habit, this last few years. He and Howard would need to make their way to Bangor again for the expert opinion of Emyr Rowlands.

"Are you ok with this son?" asked Huws. Howard merely nodded in the affirmative.

"I've another bit of news that you should know about too. They're burying Steffan on Monday week at his local Church, his parents are asking if they could have police representation there outside the Church, and due to Covid restrictions they're limited as to the number of people they can have inside, but as they have very little close family they invited me to come and maybe a couple of his close colleagues."

He looked across at Howard, who appeared deep in thought, but when he turned to face Huws, his eyes were glistening with unshed tears.

"I want to attend, of course I do, but I'm not sure I can. How can I sit there as his partner and pretend I'm just a friend?"

"I understand, but I think it is really important that you should be there for your own closure and peace of mind. Have you given any more thought to actually visiting them and telling them the truth? It isn't anything to be ashamed of. They might be a bit old fashioned, but you know, they may surprise you."

Howard, slightly shocked, was not so sure, repeating again how Steffan had said more than once that his dad in particular was homophobic, describing gay people as poofs and queers. By telling them now about their relationship, it would be like a slap in the face and quite possibly defile their image of their son.

Huws was not much of an agony aunt but fully understood that this would, bit by bit eat into Justin and erode him from the inside out beyond mending. It may even long- term cause him to feel anger towards Steffan for his lack of openness. Could he himself do some-thing about this he wondered? Then as quickly as the thought popped in his head, he pushed it back into the depths again. He shouldn't interfere, but Christ he felt for the young man sitting next to him in the passenger seat of his 'antique' car. He smiled to himself.

Howard noticed.

"Why the grin?" Huws just shook his head and smiled and told him of the conversation that he had shared with Steffan when he had driven his car. Even Justin smiled at the recollection.

"Typical Steff comment that. He was a very clever man, but in some aspects very naïve in the ways of the world."

By the time they arrived at the pathology department, they had spent a good ten minutes regaling each other with funny sayings and comments that Steffan had come out with over the time they had both known him. Huws felt that Howard's heart was just a tiny bit lighter than when they set off. He knew that could only be a tran-sient reduction in intense grief, but it was good and indeed accept-able to laugh and reminisce.

Now, to get the autopsy out of the way, he had decided on his own plan of action and hoped it would not turn out to be a terrible mistake.

It seemed that Rowlands was already well ahead with the autopsy when they both let themselves into the observation room.

His voice boomed through the speaker.

"White Caucasian male about the same age as the other two you had bought in, cause of death I would say with some confidence, catastrophic, traumatic blood loss. In my opinion, from having a propeller almost cutting him in half and severing the descending aorta going down his body. He would have been dead in no time from a traumatic cardiac arrest. The only good thing about this body is that there was a wallet with a driving license inside it, in his trouser pocket. Seems he is, that is, was local. Maybe he is a third boatman if you don't know for definite that there were only two men seen with the car and boat trailer. I believe you may now have at least a link between three of the victims, I can't imagine he would have been a random fully clothed swimmer who has got entangled with an outboard engine."

Huws answered. "Yes, we are slowly tying up some loose ends. Patrick Flint is Richard Flints nephew, another wrong one it seems, as far as Flint seniors neighbours are concerned. Wanted by the Essex force for drug related crimes and a case of ABH. Obviously had done a runner up to the North West."

"So, who was this third man then, assuming the wallet actually belonged to him, how does he fit in to the story?" asked Jane, cutting in at this point and declared that he was called James Ashley Evans and supposedly lived on the outskirts of Menai Bridge, Porthaethwy, she added the Welsh name, according to his address, if he had indeed not changed address since the license had been issued.

Huws and Howard thanked Rowlands and Jane for their time and made to leave.

"Idris, you do remember you owe me dinner, don't you?" stated Jane. "A few places are actually doing take away menus now. Maybe before the weather turns, you could treat me to a meal sitting on the wall of the Belgian prom in Menai bridge."

She winked, as Idris just looked flustered and muttered that he had not forgotten and would certainly contact her soon.

Howard took his place on the passenger seat next to him as they made to return to Llangefni station.

"I think that nice lady has a bit of a thing for you," he said with a wink. "Wasn't she the lady that caught our man on the bridge?"

"It was, but don't be daft, why would she be interested in an old bloke like me with a fat belly and unkempt hair, a male version of that TV detective Vera."

"Ha, yeah," responded Howard with a lift of his eyebrows. "I suppose you are pretty ancient," he laughed.

Huws shook his head, "You cheeky bugger." He was secretly pleased that Howard at least seemed a little more cheerful. He would have a good think today about the wisdom of his plan.

Now, they needed to return to the station and pass on the fresh information. There was also the matter of collating all the questions for a further interview with Robert Littleton who would already be going down for the cold-blooded murder of Steffan Parry, though Huws was very much afraid that his defense would get it changed to manslaughter on the basis that it wasn't premeditated. He also hoped he could somehow get more on the other deaths to definitely connect him to them and put him away for a long, long time. Knowing his luck, they would charge him with the murder and then declare double jeopardy regarding the other deaths and would throw it out at a later date, not allowing them to try him for the same crime twice. That would be a career first for him. The team had to produce more evidence and quickly.

After he finished later, he had a job to do, having just made his mind up and decided it was absolutely necessary, he would do it. He had to, for everyone's sake. He hoped to God that he was doing the right thing.

Chapter Thirty-One

HUWS HAD PHONED his mother like any good ten-year-old would have done and told her he would not likely be home for supper. Expertly deflecting her enquiry as to where he was going, she would never learn. The journey onto the mainland wouldn't take long but he decided to take his time and ponder what he would say and how he would broach the subject. Was he interfering? Would it actually make things ten times worse?

He had taken the back roads to the village of Waunfawr, the sun already setting to his right over Anglesey, its expanse stretching away from him as far as Mynydd Bodafon and Mynydd Twr which sheltered the town of Holyhead from the worst of the westerlies. The Menai Strait dividing the island from the mainland as it snaked from the Caernarfon end to Beaumaris. A complex stretch of water if local sailors were to be believed. Procrastinating was what he was doing now, he recognized it in himself, he had become a master in its art. Crawling along with thankfully no following traffic, still dithering about his task. He found the track entrance, avoiding as many potholes as he could, slowly winding his way left and right, his old car's suspension would no doubt be complaining.

He stopped outside the old house, no doubt a farmhouse at

some point in its history, the outbuildings now converted simply but tastefully into additional accommodation, holiday let maybe, or, he shook his head as he imagined the future plan may have been to accommodate Steffan and a young family. He realised that he had been holding his breath as he let out a long exhalation.

No going back now, Mrs. Parry was already in the doorway having noticed the car approach the house. Huws was convinced she had shrunk since his last meeting only a few terrible days ago, her hair unkempt atop a pale face devoid of any make up. He accepted her invitation to follow her into the house, to the same sitting room, the same armchair where he had previously dealt such a cruel blow, no doubt changing their lives forever. There was no sign of Mr. Parry.

"Come in Mr. Huws, I'm sorry the place is untidy, well-"

Huws stopped her with a raised hand. "Absolutely, nothing to worry about, I was hoping to have a bit of a chat with you both, is Mr. Parry at home?" She nodded in the affirmative.

Mrs. Parry had left the room as soon as he had discarded his coat and sat down, she reappeared with a cup of tea in a China cup on a saucer. "I apologise for not phoning you in advance, but it was a little of an impromptu decision on my behalf to drive over."

She looked him in the eye before responding.

"Yes, he is at home, but he's taken to spending all his time in his workshop, I think he's avoiding me. Men are not good you know with this sort of thing. I would swear he has lost a stone in just a few days, hardly touched any food since we were told. Are you here to talk about the funeral? We have asked for some of Steffan's friends to attend and maybe the Police service flag for thc coffin."

"Well not entirely, I believe that the funeral arrangements are in hand, his colleagues have all the details under control. I also fully understand Mr. Parry's distress; I lost my wife not very long ago. It must be harder to lose a son, it's not the natural pattern of things." He paused; Mrs. Parry had sat down alongside him, her hands wrapped in a tea towel on her lap akin to a comfort blanket.

"I'm not sure we will ever recover from this; it worries me that Guto will just close up and shut out everybody including me. The minister came to see us a couple of days after Steffan died and he refused to speak to him, God had let Steffan down he said, not protected him, taken care of him. What use was God to him now. Staunch Chapel goer all his life you see, a deacon, a lay preacher when needed. Hard for him."

Huws understood this feeling of betrayal. He himself had been raised in a Methodist Chapel, Sunday school and Band of Hope attending upbringing, though he would freely admit having not really taken all the religion stuff seriously, seeing it more as an inter-ference in his young life, stopping him from doing his hobbies. It seemed so long ago now, he barely remembered what those hobbies were. He did remember however, having to wear the stiff starched collar and dull tie throughout the day, Sundays considered a special day in his family. No playing outside during the day at all. Thank-fully as far as he was concerned, Gwen had far less time for religion than his mother was happy about. His mother had barely missed a service all through her life. It was very much the thing she missed most with the Covid lockdowns.

"I want to talk to you both about Steffan, if that is ok. It will be better if you both hear what I say." That was it, no going back now.

Mrs. Parry nodded and left the room to seek out her husband. She took a while. Huws was almost regretting his decision to spring this news onto them. A long twenty minutes later an ashen, stern faced Guto Parry had still not uttered a word. Mrs. Parry seemed mute, waiting for her husband to respond first as if what she might say was of a lesser importance and of no consequence.

Nothing was forthcoming. Guto simply stared at his clenched hands, Mrs. Parry raised her hand onto his shoulder in comfort. It was shaken off as Guto stood up and left the room. They both looked at each other as the back door slammed.

"I'm so sorry," started Huws, "maybe it was a mistake to come here and announce this, maybe I should have let things lie and not have interfered."

"No, cariad, it was the right thing to do to tell the truth. I'm not shocked, disappointed or any of those things. I'm surprised maybe, because we never guessed but I will still love my son to the ends of the earth. I'm more open minded you see; I'm just glad that he found happiness. I'm sad of course that he didn't feel able to tell us, but Guto is old fashioned and would not have liked it. Ashamed I suppose, for his own silly old-fashioned reasons, though these days people are not bothered about these things are they. I'm sure, given a few hours moping and mulling it over in his shed, he will come around. When he does, I would like to meet young Justin Howard."

"Ah right, uhm, well, he has no idea I have come to see you here today. He is totally bereft as you may well imagine. He may even be angry at my interference. He is a lovely lad, and like Steffan would surely have done, will go far in the force."

Huws got up and took both her hands in his and squeezed them gently. He felt no resistance in her response, possibly taking comfort, which she was unable to find in her husband.

"I will talk to him."

Idris Huws handed her a scribbled note with Justin's mobile number on it, nodding his thanks, he walked towards his car. Mrs. Parry could be seen watching him weave his way down the drive, as he watched her in his rear-view mirror.

His drive back home to Anglesey felt lighter, relief that he had made the right decision, but he would hold off mentioning his visit to Howard. Time would tell if his interference had been welcomed. It may take time for old Guto to accept his son's choices. He sincerely hoped he would.

His mother was watching television when he returned, intermittently glancing down at the little book in her hand to complete the Sudoku puzzle that she was addicted to, claiming that keeping her brain alert would ward off dementia. Time would tell on that score. At least she didn't ask where he had been. He chose to have a shower and an early night. It would be another day of pressure tomorrow. An important day. He needed results.

Chapter Thirty-Two

THERE WAS bustle and an electric atmosphere at the station that morning. Two important matters were to be dealt with, but first of all Huws had to await the result of the first before he could deal with the all-important interview with Robert Littleton.

A group of officers had already been sent to the home of their latest body, James Ashley Evans to see what they could come up with. He would have to be patient. He needed to notify the defendants solicitor anyway of their intention to re interview Littleton and it would be a trip out to the nearest prison where he was being held for trial and that being an hour or so away.

He chose to have a quiet sit down to pore over the information that they had up until now. It wouldn't hurt him to have a bit of a break while his very reliable team did the legwork for a while. It was all educational in his book. He looked towards the family photo on the shelf and thought to himself that quite possibly this could or in fact should be his last job. Losing Gwen had taken the wind out of his sails, along with his enthusiasm, and the loss of a good young colleague had been a hefty kick in the guts.

More than likely his home life would change now, it was doubtful his mother would ever return to her own home, or at least until this bloody awful Covid had died down. He also had the unpleasant job on Monday of attending the funeral of young Parry-such a loss to the police, he would have gone somewhere, no doubt right to the top.

His mobile rang, he didn't recognize the landline number but recognized the voice immediately. It was Mrs. Parry, she introduced herself by her first name, Eluned, almost giving him permission to do the same. "Guto would like a word with you please, if you have the time."

"Yes, yes of course, I have time now if that is convenient for him."

"Thank you, I will pass him the phone, hang on please."

There was a whispered exchange as she passed her husband the phone, Idris Huws wondered what he was going to hear. "Hello, Guto yma."

He introduced himself in his native Welsh tongue, clearly more comfortable and at ease, and Idris Huws perfectly happy to follow suit. He paused before continuing, declaring that he would like to meet young Justin Howard. That he had come to terms, with help from Eluned, with the fact that Steffan was with a man, he accepted that if his son was happy, and that it was what he wanted, then it was ok. He asked Huws to contact Justin and ask if he was indeed willing to meet them both for a chat. It would be good to meet him and have an open conversation about their son. Huws knew that this phone call would have been a hugely difficult one for him to make, Huws didn't think Gusto had it in his nature to back down, clearly Eluned had worked hard to convince him otherwise. He assured Guto he would have a word with Justin and see if he was prepared to meet. Clearly Eluned preferred not to have made the call herself.

His conversation with Justin was difficult, the young man initially shocked, he was hesitant to agree to the meeting, afraid of breaking down in front of them and worried that he would indeed be rejected out of hand, out of Steffan's life. What if they changed their minds?

With some persuasion he agreed to visit them the following evening. He said he would take some albums with him of photos they had taken on their holidays over the last few years, both having a mutual love of outdoor sports and nature. Maybe that could in some way prove to them that they were committed to their relationship and held a deep love and respect for each other.

Huws was pleased and hoped from the bottom of his heart that is may bring peace to the three of them in some way, to help with their grief. Acceptance by Guto was in itself a huge step after his brief meeting with them considering Guto's rapid departure into his shed which Huws chose not to mention.

Once again, his phone rang, this time an officer from the group that had visited James Ashley Evans's home.

There had been as expected, no one in, access had been achieved by slightly more damaging means, the house searched, the house itself was in a decent street just on the edges of Menai Bridge. It was relatively tidy, evidence of a considerable wealth if the material possessions were anything to go by. A vast array of electronic equipment, laptops, music playing devices with state-of-the-art speaker systems. A decent, almost new Mercedes convertible in the integrated garage. Reasonably stocked larder of essentials indicating a good taste, but very little food in the fridge, and what was there already decaying with mould. Green cheese, sour milk, bacon developing a green translucent wet shine within its opened packaging, edges curled and drying where exposed to the air.

A good selection of decent wines sat in a rack on the worktop, quite a connoisseur it would appear. It was generally tidy. Expensive clothes in the wardrobe, mainly designer labels and a collection of sunglasses no doubt to match whatever garment was chosen to wear. Shoes by the dozen, all immaculate and polished.

There was no evidence that anyone else lived in the house with him. A balcony ran along the front wall of the upstairs lounge, glorious views to be enjoyed of the Strait below and the Snowdonia hills beyond. The excitable spaniel bought along by its handler to seek out any drugs was now happily chewing his yellow tennis ball, having not indicated a discovery of any incriminating evidence, totally disinterested now his task was completed.

More surprising was the unexpected appearance of a very flustered lady at the front gate who seemed furious at the fact that Mr. Evans's as she called him, had his door damaged. Demanding to know what right the police had to even be there, she was taken aside and questioned by one of the senior officers at the scene. Mr. Evans, she declared was a lovely young man. Why on earth would the police want to break into his home.

The officer took her into the hallway to keep her off the road, where local rubber neckers could now be seen congregating, also to stop her interfering with the proceedings.

"Does Mr. Evans live here alone?" she was asked. "What did he do for a living?"

The lady who declared she was his twice weekly cleaner, confirmed he did live alone, though occasionally would have friends over for dinner. She would usually prepare a casserole and a dessert for such occasions to save him cooking as he was busy at work. When asked what work he did- it must be something quite rewarding to live this sort of lifestyle, she admitted that she didn't really know, but he sometimes mentioned that he needed to deliver new boats to buyers from further afield, this was something that gave cause for him to be away for sometimes days at a time until he returned from wherever he had been either by train or taxi. In a few instances he had been away for up to a couple of weeks. It wasn't her business to know, so she rarely asked.

"Does he have any family?"

"Well, I think his mother may have passed away a long time ago. I'm not sure but this may have been her home but don't quote me on that. I don't think he has much to do with his real father who lives on a farm somewhere not too far away. He never speaks of him, but he has mentioned a couple of times in passing that he was visiting him. He was raised by a stepfather, treated him exactly as if he were his own son. I think Ashley's mother separated from his father even before he was born. He never spoke about it. The only father he has known is his stepfather. A lovely man, I met him a couple of times. Died of cancer probably about five years ago now, took him in a matter of months. Ashley looked after him here at home right until the end, he was really upset, but he has lived here alone for a while now. He has modernized the décor quite a bit and turned the house layout upside down when he had the balcony built on."

"So, he sounds a decent enough guy then, would you agree?" asked the officer.

The answer was in the affirmative, and the officer believed her. Up to now they hadn't divulged the fact that James Ashley Evans was lying in the local morgue. He knew she would find out soon enough. He decided it was not his job to tell her.

"Last question before we let you go on your way; do you have any idea what his biological father is called and where we could find him?"

"I'm not sure what his first name was but I do know that Ashley went by the name Evans as opposed to his stepfathers surname, he lived on a farm somewhere in the area though he never actually did say where it was, so sorry but I can't help you any more than that."

"You've been very helpful thank you, we can get on with our enquiries now, someone will be along later to do some repairs. It will be as good as new."

"Thank you, I would hate him to come back and find a mess. I'll tidy up and do a small shop, so he has some fresh food for when he comes home."

No one wanted to tell her that she was wasting her time.

All of this information was relayed to Huws back at the office. He was still busy preparing his notes for the next interview with Littleton. There didn't seem to be much at the moment to link the Evans lad with Littleton or Flint, but it was still early days. The team would continue its search of Evans' home just in-case something appeared as a clue to all this confusion. They also needed to do some homework to find out who his birth father was and where he lived, particularly as it seemed now that he was likely the only next of kin. It would be a phone call to the local Registrar on Monday morning.

Chapter Thirty-Three

JUSTIN WAS SITTING IN A LAY-BY, just down the road from the Parry's house, trying his best to compose himself. He would, when not at work still totally lose it and become a shaking desolate weeping wreck. He had no close friends to turn to, loads of colleagues yes, but his life had always been work and Steffan. They didn't need any more than that. He was now, in his mind, totally alone.

Fearful of the reception he would be given by Steff's parents, he was wary of going and knocking on the door. They would be waiting for him, no doubt as, if not more nervous than he was at this moment. They had agreed on six o' clock, Huws, having agreed to him leaving work at four to shower and change. It was now ten to. He glanced at himself in the rear-view mirror, there was no hiding the puffiness around his eyes. He would have to do. He had a last blow of his nose and turned the ignition. He paused to check the road was clear, still wishing this was not happening. Maybe very soon he might wake from what surely must be a nightmare. Steff telling him it was all just a very bad joke.

He pulled up on the drive next to Guto Parry's car. He knew it was his, remembering Steffan telling him that his father had eventually bought himself a smaller car, a tidy Volkswagen Polo instead of the cumbersome Volvo Estate that he had kept for a hundred years, or so it had seemed to Steffan, who hadn't remembered his father having any other car. He pulled up his tie as he got out of his car, straightening the bottom of his tidy casual jumper, over his cream chinos. He had spent a good twenty minutes polishing his smart tan brogues.

Taking a breath, he approached the front door, taking in the hanging baskets that needed deadheading and watering, no doubt the neglect having happened over this last few days.

Lifting his hand up to use the brass knocker, the door was pulled open, Steffan's mother standing in the doorframe, she must have been watching through the window, wanting a first look no doubt at their late son's partner. Bottom lip quivering and puffy eyes to equal his own.

She stepped out towards him, arms wide and embraced him. He feared he would not be able to breathe, so tight was she holding onto him, then great sobs wracked her body. Justin struggled to maintain his composure, glad she didn't speak or expect him to. She released her hold, gesturing for him to enter past her as she wiped her eyes with a hanky from her pocket. She indicated towards a room to his left. Standing next to a slate-built ornately stepped fireplace, adorned with horse brasses, was Mr. Parry, a shine to his eyes indicating the early formation of a tear that he likely hoped would not drop. Justin nodded and approached him, offering his hand. It wasn't taken. He dropped it disappointingly by his side as Mr. Parry indicated towards an armchair. He feared that a homophobic lecture was to be delivered, though the phone call had not indicated that would be the case. Surely not.

"Thank you for coming to meet us lad." Almost a whisper then a cleared throat producing a more confident voice. They had both now seated themselves on the throw covered sofa at ninety degrees to him, making him have to almost sit sideways on to face them. He imagined the same furniture having been in place throughout Steffans's growing up. It made him feel somehow comforted regardless of how the conversation might pan out over the next few minutes.

He was asked how long he had been in the police force and whether he was brought up locally. He sensed this was just filling space and was proved right when Mrs. Parry took her husband's hand in her own and took over the conversation.

"You can understand cariad, that this came as a shock to us both that Steffan was you know, a homosexual, one of those gays. We had no idea, and I suppose we didn't guess anything because he was always a studious young man, spending a lot of time studying for his exams. I suppose we are very old fashioned as well and not used to the modern ways of the world. I expect possibly that he was a bit lonely living here. Sometimes a school friend would meet him, and they would often go cycling or walking together."

She paused as if watching a past memory play a cinematic version in front of her. "He loved climbing to the summit of Moel Eilio and walking the ridge towards Y Wyddfa, we just assumed that he would eventually meet a young policewoman, once he joined the force. However, we have spoken a lot about Steffan, since he died." She cleared her throat, close to tears again.

"What we mean to say is that we don't mind, don't mind at all now we are getting used to the idea. In fact, we are pleased that he wasn't alone and obviously he was very much loved by you and liked by his colleagues. We grew up in different times, but really want you to know that we are now ok with it, and in fact we are slightly sad that we maybe could have been a bigger part of your lives if Steffan had known we were more accepting than maybe we appeared to be. We are very sorry about that."

She looked from Justin towards her husband, hoping he would pick up the conversation. Justin knew this would have been harder for him to accept. He belonged to a different time, an old- fashioned upbringing. Mr. Parry nodded in agreement. Finding the words difficult to collect together, he then asked Justin if he would like to say a few words about Steffan during the funeral service and how they would both like it if he would share the front pew with them. He added that they would like to keep in touch and maybe get to hear a little of their life together.

Justin nodded, he fought back the lump of tightness in his

throat, fearing he would break down. Instead, he reached for the envelope in his pocket and handed it to Mrs. Parry who looked quizzically at him.

"These are some photographs that I had copies of, most of our photos are on our phones but we got these printed as we were going to frame them to put up in the flat. A couple of them we took when we visited the Fairy pools on the Isle of Skye, I persuaded Steff to dive under the underwater arch. He was terrified, but he was so buzzing after he managed it that he didn't stop talking about it for hours and hours.

We stayed in a lovely shoreside cottage near a little village called Applecross, there was no road to it, we had to walk in and out every day, probably a couple of miles or so each way. The other is of a holiday we took to Tromso in Norway to see the Northern lights. I thought you might like to see them. He convinced me to walk the Eilio ridge with him, I told him never to make me do it again, with all its false summits I thought we were never going to reach the top. He assured me the views would be magnificent. We sat in the round cairn at the top to eat our lunch."

Mrs. Parry was slowly passing the photographs one at a time to her husband, tears ran down both their faces, the silent tears of utter sadness and loss.

"Can we keep these?" she asked. "I'd love to frame them and put them up here in the house."

"Of course, I would love you to have them."

They both stood up, some invisible contact between them realizing that they now needed to be alone. Justin followed suit, surprised when both approached him and took him into their embrace.

"Thank you for loving our son, we were very proud of him and always will be. We are also very sorry for your loss. We would both very much like to keep in touch and hear of your life together, if you would allow us to be a small part of it."

Justin nodded, unable to speak. He went towards the front door, composing himself enough to tell them he would see them both on Monday.

He turned the key in the ignition, Mrs. Parry watched him manouver his car around theirs, and he could still see her standing desolate as he exited the gate.

Pulling into the same lay-by that he had been parked in, no more than an hour before, he released all the tension that had bottled up to bursting inside him, he screamed and sobbed, bereft, broken. Head down thumping the steering wheel all the pent up hard controlled emotion bursting out. Even he was shocked at its ferocity. He howled and bawled, not even caring that someone may park up nearby.

He didn't know quite how long he had sat there, but somehow; he'd managed to fall asleep. The worry about meeting Steff's parent had caused a couple of sleepless nights, though, in truth, he wasn't sure whether he had actually slept much at all since that awful day when he had held him in his arms as he watched his very life leaving his eyes. The dreams, or more like nightmares had been vivid, most of them involving Steff. Would he ever be able to picture him in normal times again? He worried that amongst all his anguish that he had not told Steff that he loved him as he lost him. A stupid recognition of being at work preventing him uttering those words, oh how he regretted it.

Justin was not sure where he was going to go from here, he wasn't actually sure as to whether he actually wanted to go on at all. He rested his head on the steering wheel, knowing he had to make a move. A speech needed preparing for the funeral service. Thinking about it now, he wondered what the hell had entered his head to even agree to do it in the first place. He rubbed his eyes, sore and puffy from crying, turned the ignition and made to go home. He had decided to shower and change and go back to work, anything had to be better than sitting alone in the house surrounded by 'their' possessions. There had to be something he could be getting on with, anything that would see Littleton behind bars for a very long time. He remembered very little of the journey home, likely he should not even have been driving.

Chapter Thirty-Four

THE SEARCH TAKING place in Ashley Evans's house had not been particularly fruitful for the experienced team. A thorough trawl had however come across a small brown notebook in a bedside drawer which could well shine a light on some of it, a list of names written in a good clear hand, almost in itself an indication of good education, Ricky F, Patrick F, Kyle and Rob.

All familiar names, the only name missing being his own. They had linked Littleton to the others if he was indeed the noted Rob. Huws had cursed when he was told of the discovery that it was just 'Rob' and not Robert or even Rob L. It was however a positive start. There was not a lot of content to the note in all honesty, just figures and a date. Coincidentally the date of the first incident and the death of Richard Flint.

Huws had taken a look through the book, carefully gloved. This could in fact be an important piece of evidence. He totted up the figures in his head, if these numbers were related to grams of Cocaine it would be interesting to double check on the amount of Cocaine found in Richard Flint's car boot, which just happened to have been found in the same location as Robert Littleton.

That haul had been in multiple packages. He bought the case

details up on the screen in front of him, he hated damned computers. He could just about, after years of trying, find his way around the basics but still had to admit to calling on the help of one of the youngsters on the team if he was stuck.

He scrolled through and sure enough his reckoning of eight thousand grams meant there was a missing two thousand grammes somewhere to add to the six thousand grammes of Cocaine found in the car. Hmm, he wondered where that could have got to, still a high street value to it. He would worry about that later.

Other notes in the book related to boat deliveries that Evans had clearly made over the last few years. Cardiff to Liverpool, Portugal to Cork, Campbelltown to Belfast amongst many, many others, he was quite the sailor. All the boats were named and described, length, beam, cruiser, pleasure, racers, all classified either A, B, C, D, according to the notes which meant nothing to Huws. Was he innocently involved in transporting boats between owners or was there more to it?

He needed to get someone checking up on these individual boat owners just in case there was more to this, he would get the most recent ones checked, the older ones may well have been sold on again or even sunk as far as he would know.

"Griff," he called, loudly enough that the young PC came scuttling through.

He was given his task of chasing up some ownership details and whether any of them had any previous, or in fact, current drugs charges against them. He asked PC Griff Edwards to get onto the banks, to ask for statements relating to Evans' finances over the last at least five years. His transporting business or whatever the marine term might be, was clearly lucrative going by the contents of his house. He also told the crew next door to chase up the whereabouts of Evans's father.

A fair few loose ends needed to come together now. Littleton was awaiting trial and he wanted all the facts before the interview next week, which was organized for straight after the funeral on Monday. He was going to be put away regardless, but he wanted to be sure he didn't get away with anything. Justin Howard put his head around the door.

"Sir, anything I can be getting on with this evening? I'd rather be doing something," he asked, clearly having put the idea of writing his speech out of his head.

"Sit down," Huws pointed to a chair, not having the heart to tell the young man in front of him to go home. He knew exactly how he was feeling; he had also been exactly the same. Anywhere other than home, especially once his mum had moved in with them. "But not before you have grabbed us both a coffee." He explained he would then get him caught up with today's findings. He heard the audible sigh of relief, as Howard subconsciously expressed his grate-fulness at not being sent home again.

His phone rang just as Howard returned with two steaming cups of 3 in 1 in powdered coffees. He wondered who the hell in the office had come up with the bright idea of bulk buying the vile stuff, but it was better than nothing.

"Hello?" he replied a little gruffly as he reached for his cup and promptly spilled some of it onto the desk, splashing his keyboard. Howard was onto it within seconds grabbing a handful of tissues from the man-sized box on the bookshelf.

"Sorry, who is it again?" asked Huws, less aggression in his voice this time. "Jane? Oh Jane, sorry I didn't recognize your voice for a second there, lots going on at this end as you might imagine," a pause, presumably to allow her to get a word in edgeways. "Uhm, yes, no harm in that I suppose. Thank you, yes three o clock should be fine. Do I need to bring anything along? Ok thank you."

He put the phone down, a tad flustered. Howard looked at him, raising his eyebrows questioningly.

"All ok Sir?"

"Uhm, yes, yes of course, that was Jane."

"Oh, the lady that helped trap Littleton, that Jane?" enquired Howard.

"Yes, that Jane."

Howard grinned to himself, it was like getting blood out of a stone, he waited to see what Huws would say. He knew better than to be nosey.

"She has asked me to meet her tomorrow, down by the Belgian Prom in Menai Bridge, for an outdoor picnic, apparently there are lots of Red squirrels to be seen there."

"Well, there you go then. It will do you the world of good," he declared graciously, knowing now, exactly how his boss must have felt when he lost his wife so suddenly.

He felt a slight guilt that none of them in the team had ever mentioned his wife in conversation- after the funeral, in fact none of them had attended it. Now it was almost as if it had never happened. He couldn't ever imagine himself being ready to take such a step in the future.

He perched his bottom on the corner of a table, drank his over-sweet weak coffee, and thought about anything he could, other than Steff, he was always so close to the edge.

"You all right son?" asked Huws.

"Yes, thanks, but, you know, I can't imagine now how you coped when you lost your wife, you just seemed to carry on as if nothing had happened. We all said that you had come back to work too quickly."

Huws appreciated that it had taken some guts to ask this very question, recognising that he needed to be very careful as to how he approached its response.

"Well, you see, you sort of build a bloody big wall around your-self. No one tells you what to do, it just happens, and you don't let anyone in, or any of your own emotions out. The wall is built, around a huge hole, your daily challenge appears to be to remove the bricks one by one and let other people in to help you climb out, and more importantly not to fall in that hole more than you can help. I couldn't do that see; it has taken a long time for me to just take a bit of that wall down. You sort of become two separate people, the man doing his work, and the man in his own head and private space at home and I, for example can only cope if I keep the two separate."

He looked at Howard, "It's going to take a long time, grief and the loss of someone you love dearly never goes away, it gets just a bit easier day by day, but it doesn't go away completely, don't let anyone tell you it does. Most people who tell you that, have absolutely no idea, it just takes a very slightly different position within your life. Some things will bring it back in your conscience as if your loss was the day before.

You'll find your own way through this, and people will want to help you. Let them. I didn't. It's always much harder to seek it out months down the line, when other people think you are ok and don't like to dig up old topics.

I would like to sit with you and the Parry's on Monday at the funeral if I may and remember my door will always be open for you. I don't want you to get lost down that big hole."

"Thank you, Sir. I appreciate it."

Howard kept his head down, sadness emanating from every pore of his very soul. Unwilling to allow the brimming tears to escape his eyelids.

"I have no living parents and Steff was really all I had and wanted. Because we didn't tell anyone at work it made it difficult to invite any of the team to the flat, so we just kept ourselves to ourselves really."

His voice becoming small and slightly strangled, he cleared his throat and added.

"I really don't know where I go from here Sir."

"Well one day at a time lad, one day at a time, let's get the funeral behind us and we can work out a plan, ways to move forwards. Between us all we need to get this monster behind bars then we can see where it takes you, but I repeat, I'm here behind you every step of the way in case you fall, and be sure that if you do, I will be behind you to pick you up and if I see fit, I might actually be giving you a kick up the jacksy too if necessary."

A glimmer of a smile appeared on Howards lips, he wiped away a tear as he thanked his senior officer and took the remains of his cup of coffee away with him, no doubt to pour down the nearest sink.

Chapter Thirty-Five

YOUNG PC GRIFF EDWARDS left the Llangefni incident room in the early hours of the morning. He had trawled the internet all night basically for yacht and owner information. He had whizzed off a few e mails to people that looked at first sight as being totally genuine boaty people as he referred to them. He had been told that you certainly needed a license to sail the inland waters of the UK, but not so the sea, most responsible competent sailors who did venture off the coast would likely have a day skipper license through the Royal yachting association.

He had also discovered that young Evans had actually got an International Certificate of Competence which allowed him to sail European waters, so he seemed quite legit. Obviously the individual yacht owners that he delivered to need not all be drug barons or whatever they might be called, they may just be people who chose to spend their disposable income on a boat and employed Evans to deliver the boat to them, if the purchase was made from a considerable distance away.

Whether he was using the transport to move drugs around was something, that as yet , he had not been able to prove one way or another.

His only idea to progress, was to trace the last yacht that he delivered and get a drug search dog on board just in case there were any traces on it anywhere, the only plus side to this, was that particular yacht seemed to have been delivered to Abersoch, fairly local, named The Temptress. He would phone the harbour master down there in the morning, well it was officially morning, but he doubted that they would be working at 3am. It would be his first job later on. Now he needed a few hours' sleep.

A few miles down the road Idris Huws was awake, he had heard the old clock downstairs chime every hour since he went to bed. So much on his mind. He was pleased that a few aspects of the case were coming together, his team were keen, enthusiastic workers, no doubt, he imagined, an extra determination due to the cold blooded, tragic killing of young Steffan. They had all liked him, he got on with everyone. On one hand always the one with the jokes and quips, but on the other, deadly serious, with his work a number one priority. He could have imagined him being high up the ranks in a decade or so.

A sad waste of life carried out by the scum of the earth. His hatred for Littleton was enough to upset his stomach, and certainly cause this insomnia.

His conversation with Justin today had, to an extent done him a little good, a form of counselling in reverse he supposed. Even though the emphasis was on the young man, it had been cathartic to express how he had felt when he lost his Gwen. He reached across to her side of the bed, knowing full well she wouldn't be there to take his hand and give it a sleepy squeeze.

Today, as it was by now, he was meeting Jane for this picnic. What should he wear he thought? There had been no real need to consider his clothing for a while now, Covid and the loss of Gwen had cut his wardrobe down to a couple of ties, a trio of work shirts, an equal number of trousers and underwear, oh, and his tidy sports jacket. Smart casual, he supposed, he would have a scout about in the wardrobe. Telling his mum had been a no no, he didn't want her making more of it than what it was, and certainly at the moment he was not going to mention it to Elin. He would just tell them that he was going to interview someone regarding work.

It was five a.m. near as dammit when Idris eventually gave up trying to sleep, he quietly got dressed and sneaked down the stairs, the dog surprised to see him, thwacking his tail enthusiastically against a kitchen cabinet.

"Shh, come over here." He quickly threw some water over his face and grabbed a nearby tea towel to wipe himself dry. Gwen would have told him off for that.

Grabbing the excited dog's lead, he left by the back door, quietly closing it behind him and pocketing the key. Thankfully Ben the old dog was not much of a barker so they both wandered off as a pair enjoying the silence of the predawn stillness. Not even the birds it seemed, had woken up yet.

Chapter Thirty-Six

THREE HOURS later Huws was in the incident room as were most the team. PC Griff Edwards was having a long conversation with someone on the phone, everyone had their heads down. It was supposed to be his day off, not that he really took them when they were working on a case anyway. It was an unspoken rule that the team worked through and took their rest when they could.

Being at home today would just have jangled his nerves more than they already were. He had packed a bag of clothes to change into, had a towel, his charged-up shaver and an old bottle of after-shave that he had found. Did these things go sour with time he wondered? It seemed to smell ok when he had randomly pressed the plunger. He knew this was just a casual meeting with Jane this after-noon, as far as he was concerned, he still needed to show he had at least made a bit of an effort.

Edwards entered his office, sniffing as he came in, no doubt picking up the waft of tester Aftershave but choosing it best to ignore it.

"Sir, last night I did some work on the boats, ehm, yachts, some big posh yachts that Evans had been moving around. Most of the journeys seem to have been legitimate deliveries as far as I can tell, and it is an actual job. He had the qualifications and the experience it seems to have been able to do this. Quite a lucrative job in itself. Pays very well.

The only thing I obviously couldn't really get into with the owners was the obvious question of whether they suspected their yacht of having been used for the transportation and moving of drugs."

He paused to take a breath!

"I have taken the liberty Sir, of phoning the harbourmaster at Abersoch to see if he can give us the contact details of the new owner of a yacht that was the last yacht that he delivered. It was sailed down from Leith waterfront near Edinburgh, all around the North Coast of Scotland then down the West Coast, sailing between the West Coast and the Outer Hebrides. And eventually down to Abersoch. No mean journey in a yacht, though the harbourmaster did say that he would have no doubt have been under engine power most of the time. Using engine power also meant that in anything other than the superyachts, they could be sailed alone.

He said the journey details should be in the daily log on the yacht, usually in a fair amount of detail. He also said that there were a few possible stop off points along the way where he may have moored up for the night or even refueled. In order of distance sailed each day, he reckoned the sorts of places he may have stopped may be." He looked at his notebook and continued, "Aberdeen, Inverness, Thurso, then possibly making for Stornoway on Lewis. Seems there is a worrying drug culture up there now with Glaswegian dealers targeting the local youth. Maybe then Tobermory, Campbelltown, Belfast then a final run down over a couple of days to Abersoch".

Huws looked at him in awe.

"Bloody hell, you have been busy. What is the gist of where this is going though?"

Impressive he thought.

"Well Sir, it turns out that this yacht is on a sling, in the inner harbour and hasn't moved or been put to sea because of Covid. The owner hasn't even had the opportunity to step foot on it yet. The last person to have actually been on the boat will certainly have been Evans. The harbourmaster," another glance at his notes "Gwilym Williams, is going to contact the owners this morning to see if we can get a team on board and a drug dog. He will get back to me as soon as he has word. I have told him though Sir, that it would be nice to have permission, but likely we would do this anyway, permission or not, Uhm, do we need a warrant to search a boat?"

"Well, you have got me there lad, I will check up on it, but I do know that the Coastguard survey officers can do spot checks on boats so it must be legal. Let's see if we get permission first. But exemplary work. Well done. Just keep me notified and hopefully we will have joined all the dots sooner rather than later now."

Edwards nodded his appreciation and made to leave the room, stepping back to allow PC Rogers to enter.

"Mm, that's a nice smell, which one of you is wearing aftershave today then?" Edwards winked at her and indicated his head towards DI Huws who had become quite red.

"What can I do for you?" asked Huws.

"Well actually, I've been contacting the local registry office. The admin there were good enough to go in yesterday, although they are closed due to Covid and working from home. They have been through the appropriate records and it seems that James Ashley Evans's father is listed as a William Huw Evans who farms in Allt Goch, well at least he lives in a farmhouse at Allt Goch. A few phone calls this morning have discovered that he lives in a house on the land but that another local now rents the land off him and farms it himself.

I was given a contact number for that person and he says that Ashley Evans as far as he was aware had barely visited his estranged father all through his childhood, but during the last year he had seen him drive onto the yard, always in the same flash car, but never staying long. He had watched him one day literally go into one of the sheds, and not even knocked his father's door. He didn't think they had much to say to each other. He had heard them shouting loudly and angrily on more than one occasion. No love lost there I suspect."

"Good, good, we may be making good progress, that's what I like to hear." he responded, glancing at his watch.

"The only thing I might suggest now is that we sit on this until after the funeral tomorrow. I don't want anything major kicking off until then, but we will need to potentially get a team down to Abersoch on Monday afternoon, I doubt the boat will be going anywhere anytime soon. At the same time if we have enough manpower, a couple of officers or three, down to Evan Senior's farm to have a look and see if we find anything interesting."

"Yes Sir," acknowledged Rogers.

"No one is looking forwards to tomorrow, but everyone is organized now to give Steff a proper send off."

Idris Huws nodded his response.

"Thank you, you are all doing a splendid job."

Time was slowly ticking on, he decided to get some fresh air to wake himself up a bit and a takeaway coffee in the little shop in the high street. By the time he got back it would be time to change and set off to meet Jane. He was quite looking forwards to it. Part of him however, worried about the consequences. He wasn't sure he wanted this to develop into anything more at the moment. He acknowledged to himself that he got on well with her, albeit in the brief meetings through their work. She was pleasant and easy to rub along with, as well as being intelligent and a good conversation was to be had with her. Anyway, he needed to get on. He would just see how they got on and treat it as a casual meeting between work colleagues. It was for the best. For now.

Chapter Thirty-Seven

JUSTIN WAS AWAKE WELL before his phone alarm rang, in fact he wasn't sure whether he had slept at all. He had put on a podcast as he went to bed but could not for the life of him recount what it was about, so he must have slept at least for a while, but that horrible type of exhausting sleep where you feel that you are completely awake.

He hated the silence now, the quietness of the room as he settled to sleep, no gentle breathing next to him, or the odd utterance of words during a vivid dream. Even the odd snore. Just nothing. The last few nights he had taken to putting the podcasts that were downloaded onto his phone to 'noise the quiet' if there was such a saying.

He threw the quilt back, it needed changing, although he was reluctant to do so, as it still smelt slightly of Steffan, or at least his shower gel. His clothes were still on the bedroom chair on his side-his chairdrobe as Steff called it. Washed clothes waiting to be put away underneath the most recently worn. Nothing was persuading him at the moment to put them away or worse still, give them to charity. Steff was to be buried in his full uniform, he had already the other day taken a white shirt and tie to the undertaker along with his best dress uniform. Taking his time to polish his boots, bulling the toes to a bright shine, to be told that they may not use them. Not always a regular practice, that had slightly thrown him, but he had insisted. His own polished parade boots stood alone.

He showered, suddenly again overwhelmed with loss, he cried like a baby as the hot water ran over his head and down his quaking tormented body. He supported himself with his hands against the wall. He still didn't believe this could actually be real, at times expecting Steff to come through the door.

His legs gave under him as he slithered down the glass screen and curled up pathetically helpless to control himself. Every night as he fell asleep, he would see Steff's face in those last moments of his life, a look of surprise, disbelief, disappointment even, as he stared up at Justin, followed quickly by emptiness in those beautiful star-tlingly green eyes of his. Was that sight going to haunt him for the rest of his life like some terrible recurring nightmare? He remem-bered thinking that the shade of green couldn't possibly be real, that they must be coloured contact lenses. He had noted though that his dear mother had exactly the same albeit slightly dulled by age, and now permanently dulled by sadness. No parent should lose a child. He had only known Steff just over a handful of years, they on the other hand had raised him and enjoyed every milestone along the way. It was terrible for them, and now they had admitted him into their life despite their hurt and loss and despite them not having been open with them about their relationship and deep love for each other.

Was his grief going to remain this overpowering for forever more? It was exhausting and cruel and incredibly potent in its power over him.

Exhausted, he dried himself and laid out his best suit on the bed. He had ironed his shirt last night. Steff would have laughed at his efforts. He had always taken on the task of ironing, Justin had laughed at his insistence that even underpants and socks needed doing, well-taught by his mother Eluned before he went away to training school he claimed. His own attempt today was just about passable. Steff was quite envious that Justin discarded the uniform as soon as he joined the CID, he was very much into his designer clothes and to a degree chose what Justin wore day to day to keep him looking 'smart'.

A few miles away Idris Huws was replicating Justin's actions as far as showering and dressing was concerned. Being CID, he was not uniformed and had not been for a fair while, Justin would be the same. He knew the other attending officers would be uniformed and would line the roadside approaching the Church to form a guard of honour.

The undertaker would have set up speakers outside in the cemetery so that everyone outside could hear the service.

Whilst dressing, he thought back to yesterday afternoon, spending a couple of hours with Jane Mathews, he had enjoyed the company. They had walked around Church Island and through the little woodland before finding a spot to sit on the promenade wall to enjoy a picnic that Jane had prepared.

They had managed to talk about all sorts once they got the inevitable work chatter out of the way. She was easy to get along with, they had a liking of walking and dogs in common, and good meals in decent restaurants.

Idris tried his hardest not to think of his Gwen, feeling it would intrude on their enjoyment, but also a hint of guilt would pop up out of the blue as if she were watching them and tapping him on the shoulder, that made him feel a bit of a traitor to her memory.

They had ended the afternoon planning a walk on the mainland along the lake near Beddgelert. He would enjoy that, he had not been there with Gwen and Elin, so there would be no familiar memories. Jane told him to bring Ben his dog as she would be bringing her terrier along for the walk and they may as well introduce them she said with a wink. They planned to end their walk with a cup of something hot at Gwynant café.

She did however catch him out with a peck on the cheek. He had pathetically nodded and stupidly taken her hand to shake as they split to walk to their respective cars. She must think he was a total buffoon.

Justin was just telling himself off for procrastinating, messing about wasting time, putting off the inevitable of leaving for the church. Randomly flicking between Facebook, Twitter and Instagram without actually absorbing anything he was seeing on his phone screen. He wasn't much into social media, that had been Steff's domain, always interested in what people around him were doing.

The ringing phone jolted him back to the here and now. It was Eluned Parry. Did he want to meet them at the undertaker's Chapel of Rest and travel behind the hearse to the Church? They were going to say a last goodbye to Steff before the coffin was permanently closed. He couldn't speak, the words stolen out of his mouth before taking on any form. Christ, did he want to? Could he actually bear to do that? He mumbled a few words no doubt incoherently in response to the poor woman and said he would make his way there. He knew it would have taken a lot for her to phone and ask.

Taking a big breath, he switched off the call, and at the same time put his phone on silent. He had to set off, there were no more excuses. It had to be done. He glanced in the hallway mirror as he made for the door, a gaunt grey face looking back at him, but at least with tidy hair. It would have to do. Maybe it would help him lay the ghost of that awful vision of Steff's face. He turned the key in the lock behind him and strode towards their car. He dreaded what he was expected to face in the next couple of hours. He so wished Steffan could be there to tell him to just grow a pair and get on with it and not be such a wuzz as was his habit.

Huws had made his way directly to the Church, he was pleased to see a good turnout of officers awaiting the warning that the hearse was on its way. Subdued voices chatted, until Huws appeared as did the DCI, who had wanted to attend.

Cars had been parked on roadside verges along the approaches, pushed up against the hedges to allow free passage of the hearse along the lane.

Justin once again bottled it and pulled in to a layby before he reached the Chapel of Rest at the local funeral home. He realised he would need to put his big girl pants on and do what he could to support Steff's parents, who were likely just as scared as he was of this step. He also knew that if he did not take this opportunity, he would likely regret it for the rest of his life. It had to be done. He started the engine and drove the last mile down the road. The Parry's car was already there, they would be travelling in a funeral car to the Church. Justin walked to the door to be greeted by a black suited thin featured, grey- complexioned man, he thought to himself that they couldn't have found a more suitable looking man for the job than this one. He nodded an acknowledgement as he waved his hand towards the entrance door.

Justin had never been in such a place before, he wasn't sure what to expect, but found himself pleasantly surprised at the light, airy, flower-decorated room to which he was led. Guto and Eluned Parry both stood up to greet him, both masked as was he. He hated it, hiding people's faces, but not to be hidden was the hurt emanating from their eyes. They took his hands in theirs, the three of them for a long moment joined in their grief, unspeaking but fully under-standing.

The gaunt man nodded his head and asked if they were ready. A glance at each other and an affirming nod of their heads. They walked ahead; arms entwined in mutual support. He followed breathing deeply to allay tears. He stood back as they both looked down at their son. Justin, unable yet to look, fearing that same look of surprise and shock would be there for him to see all over again. Mrs. Parry reached towards him and wrapped a loving arm around his middle and drew him closer, his eyes tightly shut. She squeezed him gently and he opened his eyes to see Steff, the Steff he loved, unblemished, beautiful, handsome chiseled features. Those gorgeous long lashes and high cheekbones that he had fallen in love with. His dark hair just showing a few grey hairs above his ears, distinguished Steff had described them. It took his breath away. Mrs. Parry took his hand and placed it gently onto Steffan's porcelain white hand and nodded at him to stay as they both left dignified and stoic beyond belief. He wanted to hug him, hold him close, he instead stroked his face, brushed his fingers along his lips and as the tears flowed- told him he would always love him. The gaunt man appeared and took him through to the entrance room. The Parry's were escorted into the funeral car, and once ensconced, Steffan's coffin was rolled out of a side door and placed carefully into the open back of the hearse, covered by a police drape, tasteful bouquets of flowers arranged either side. The last object placed on the coffin broke Justin's heart, almost taking the legs from under him as they placed his helmet on the top of the coffin.

Chapter Thirty-Eight

THE TEAM RETURNED to work almost immediately after the funeral, which had gone as well as these things could. Justin had delivered a beautiful speech, unprepared and from the heart. The odd hesitation of desperate composure, his colleagues smiling encouragingly at him from their socially distanced positions across the church. Thankfully no singing was allowed of the hymns chosen by his mother, no choking of their throats with the threat of tears being held back. Justin would have liked to have played a little part in the choice of music, because hymns were certainly not Steff's bag. He understood however that they knew nothing of his likes and dislikes and most eclectic tastes in music- Il Silenzio and Barcarolle being just two of his favourites, surprising perhaps in a man his age. The Parry's had dealt unasked with all the registration of death and the officialdom which follows a loss. Justin was at least reconciled that it was a burden that he did not have to involve himself with.

No hand shaking was allowed outside the church, merely, masked utterances of condolence towards the three bereft people standing outside the main door, some with no words, merely a nod of the head in acknowledgement of their loss.

Steff's internment in the quiet graveyard an almost silent affair other than the sacred words by the parish vicar. Justin was encouraged to take a handful of soil to drop into the grave followed by a white rosebud handed to him by Eluned. He stood aside silently as the few people there followed suit, not daring to make eye contact with anyone lest he broke up. He had said his goodbyes to Guto and Eluned who begged that he please keep in touch. He assured them that he would.

Huws had driven Justin home but no doubt, they would both be in the incident room later. Looking for work to deflect the inner torment in their heads. Justin from his very new, barely accepted loss and Huws' from his freshly exposed memories of his own loss.

Voices were subdued but there was a palpable frizzon of excitement as the team renewed their determination to get their colleague and friends killer behind bars, preferably for the rest of his life.

By mid-afternoon a drugs team had been detailed to go to check over The Temptress in Aberdaron. The harbourmaster had contacted the owners who were fully compliant about the search albeit a tad shocked as to the reasoning.

Huws would await news of any results, then tomorrow as agreed and planned, they would go and talk to the father. Likely they wouldn't get much from there, particularly if it was not a particularly good relationship between father and son, but it would make sure all bases were covered. He wanted all the information he could get together in the bag before he was to face Littleton again.

Standing at his office doorway, he wondered why the designers of the new build had bothered to put doors in the new building, it was like having his own space within a huge glass fish-tank, there was only one full wall in his office at all and that had the window in it with a grey view overlooking the County council offices and the police car park. He preferred the isolation and privacy of his own room in the old station, not a million miles from where he was now, even with its browning paintwork from years of smoking police officers inhabiting the space, but it had a sort of familiar comfort to it. Modern wasn't always good.

His team were busy, he knew the station's future would be in safe hands after his retirement, keen and enthusiastic, not yet soured by the realities of the dark side of the world, however he was certain that was partly due to the loss of Steffan.

The Perspex panel in the main room was now covered in photos, so many it looked like the National gallery. Lines criss- crossing, joining people together. Out alone on the right-hand side was a photo of Steffan, no doubt taken at his passing out parade, no red drawn lines had been drawn to join him to any of the others, no doubt the team being reluctant to associate their friend and colleague with the rest that they considered villains.

He moved through the team, towards the little kitchen, adjoining a reasonably comfortable rest room. There wasn't even a kettle, just a wall boiler especially set for hot drinks. He added a sachet of the two in one coffee, sachets that he had purchased himself that afternoon on the way in. That three in one stuff was vile, sickly sweet. He stirred his cup on the way back through to his office to dissolve every possible little milky lump that might rise to the top. He hid the packet in the back of the wall cupboard out of sight, for maybe a while if he was lucky.

He was stopped in his tracks mid stir by a burst of information delivered by young Rogers who had just come off the phone, obviously by the contents, it was a call from a drugs team member from Abersoch.

No actual drugs had been picked up by the dogs which was really as expected, Evans had not been expected to have left any of his haul on board any of these vessels, they were clearly a mode of transport for him. However, the dog had indicated that there had been drugs in the vessel at some point in time, just by its perseverance and enthusiasm. Better still though, said Rogers, she had been looking at the various pick up points where Evans had picked up the yachts. She and Griff had done a fair bit of homework in the last hour or so since she got in, contact had been made with the harbour master at Leith, Edinburgh to ask him if there was CCTV around the harbour, waterfront area, and yes, it seemed there were a few cameras. He had been sent a photo image of Evans, enabling him to trawl through a weeks' worth of footage, before the date that we knew the yacht arrived in Aberdaron, and he had called back.

He found footage of who we can only presume was Evans arriving there and getting onto the yacht. Probably arrived in the city by train and got a bus down to Leith.

He seemed to have a small rucksack with him, probably just clothes for the journey. However, he suggested that I should then contact the harbourmaster's or even Coastguard operations Centre's along his likely route and ask the same thing.

He was kind enough to give me a rough time plan of stopovers in suitable harbours and marinas en route, the same more or less as our local guy in Abersoch suggested. He even gave me a few relevant phone numbers that I may need. I've made some calls and unless he stopped somewhere unusual, we should be able to track him. The Leith harbourmaster has also offered to go back over a special tracker for shipping that people use. I just have to wait now to see what comes of it. I did stress that it was urgent.

Huws thanked her, hoping that the information would be with them fairly quickly. This was becoming a fair jigsaw by now. They had their man on a murder charge, but could they get him on what was borderline mass murder. Maybe that was pushing it a bit he thought to himself, but certainly four more deaths may well be of his making. This was fair progress for the day. He certainly did not want it to become a bloody case of double jeopardy.

Justin Howard had not returned to work that afternoon. More than likely exhausted. Huws decided to call it a day himself, telling his team to do the same, it had been a hard day. Unless another body turned up, then the loose ends they were working on could wait until the morning. Griff and Rachel Rogers both refusing to leave lest they had some Coastguard feedback from up north.

He would drive by Howards house on his way home and check up on the lad. From experience he knew it was so easy to shut yourself away with your thoughts, particularly after the funeral, as others seemingly got on with their lives carrying on as if nothing had happened. People that were not directly involved soon forgot another's loss. In fact, he was fully appreciative that it was draining at times to be constantly in the company of another person's grief. It could suck your emotions dry.

Laptops were closed down, paperwork folded into their files and desks left tidy. Normally there could be resistance to the 'go home' order, today was different, everyone needed some time to reflect. He knew they would be back fresh and ready to go again in the morning.

Huws visited the local Aldi, something that he had never really had to do in his life prior to Gwen's death. He filled the smaller trolley with stuff that he thought he might need if he lived alone, with a few treats thrown in there too. He put the packed bags into the boot and made his way to see Howard.

Justin was slow to answer the door, unquestioning, he invited Idris in. Idris found the kitchen and put the bags on the worktops. The place was immaculate.

"Wow, you are clearly a better housekeeper than I would ever be." A hint of a smile appeared on Justin's grey pinched face.

"Steff, hated mess, he always insisted the place was kept tidy, it was how he was with everything. I used to accuse him of having OCD when it came to cleaning, but he insisted that if the place was kept clean and tidy all the time then we could spend any days off we had together doing nice stuff. It made sense at the time."

"Do you need to take some time off lad? You can just take your time and get yourself together," added Huws.

"You didn't take any time off Sir," was the response.

"Hindsight maybe I should have. I buried my feelings in my work. I can see now that it wasn't a good thing to do." Justin looked at him, almost through him.

"I can see that, but you know, hindsight is a wonderful thing. I understand why you did that. I am scared of what this silence here might do to my head. Being at work keeps me amongst my work family and will keep me on the right track." Huws nodded; he wasn't in a position to disagree with him.

"Ok, but maybe when we have put this case to sleep, if you could bear it, we both like walking in the hills. Maybe we could rent a cottage in the lakes for a long weekend and just have a boy's weekend away? Walking, some decent meals in a restaurant, a few beers?"

"Ha, yes Sir, I think I would like tha. A change of scenery, but only as long as you do your share of cooking and washing up. Do I have to become part of your Covid bubble? I'm sure tongues would be wagging twenty to the dozen too. I suppose it would be like spending a weekend with my dad, or maybe people will think I've got myself a sugar daddy." They both laughed at this joke. Light relief at this point in time much appreciated by them both.

"You know lad, at the moment I don't really care what people think. I believe it would do us both a world of good, maybe help us both move on in whichever direction life chooses to take us.

Now get this shopping put away, I hope to God you aren't vegetarian, or one of those vegans because you might well be very disappointed in my choice of groceries."

Huws drove home somehow feeling a little lighter, as if the weight of the world that sat fairly and squarely on his shoulders for the last couple of years, had lost a little of its tonnage.

Chapter Thirty-Nine

HUWS SLEPT WELL THAT NIGHT. He had walked old Ben for an hour and eaten a hearty meal that his mother had been pleased to cook for him. Elin had even graced them with her presence in the lounge instead of shutting herself away from the world in her bedroom. Guilt tugged at Idris's heart as he oft forgot that his beautiful teenage daughter who was, day by day becoming a lovely young woman- had also lost her mum, at an age where she likely needed her the most. They had sat and watched general light rubbish on TV, thankfully his mum managed to avoid asking questions relating to work, just randomly discussing the possibility of another Covid lockdown and the apparent rise in numbers because people were basically not doing as they were told. His old mum had always been a stickler for rules.

His phone rang at seven-thirty in the morning, just as his brain was started to awaken to the sounds of the light road traffic outside. It was young Rogers, a scatter gun of information hitting his slowly alerting brain.

The harbour master from Stornoway had got back to her as had the one from Leith. He had tracked his journey day by day, stop by stop until Evans arrived at Abersoch, but CCTV footage from

Stornoway picked up Evans leaving the yacht, and meeting someone at the ferry terminal who gives him a rucksack then drives away, the monitor isn't watched all the time as they generally just have ferry vehicles and foot passengers but, the police there have taken an interest in the footage as well. It seems the man handing him the rucksack is a dealer known to them that they have been keeping an eye on as a suspected supplier on the islands and just haven't been able to catch him at his illegal trade. They would be extremely pleased to have him caught and off the island.

"Unless we hear from anyone else on his route then it's likely we have found where he made his pick up on this journey. We had clearly done the Highlands and Islands police a favour.

Now how he fits in with Littleton, Flint and the others is something we need to work out."

"Good work." Said Huws, "The early bird catches the worm and all that."

"Yes Sir, and we have a local team ready to go this morning to see Ashley Evans's father to see if they can turn anything up there".

He had a shower, dressed and left for work, breakfast would have to wait, today might just be the day when some of the pieces would come together. At last.

The team were already in when he arrived, four officers having already made their way to Evans seniors' farmstead. Time would deliver information from that direction. Huws wanted a bit of time on his own now to collate all the information in his head.

Who was responsible for what? Who was the organizer? Was there a previous connection between the four deaths? Obviously, he didn't include Steffan in this, other than having been caught in the crossfire.

He understood by now that drug dealers were driven by greed, though in this case having had local police searching the homes of all concerned, there was not much evidence of rich living. The only person who seemed to have benefitted materially from all this seemed to be Ashley Evans, though clearly, he didn't keep any of his drug hauls at home.

Was there someone else that they as yet had not discovered who pulled Evans's strings, someone who paid him well to do the sailing and picking up drugs aspects, of his part in it all?

Maybe that person would never be found. There was a tendency in organized crime of this sort for the slimy worms involved to just disappear underground for a period of time, sometimes years only to find another lackey with greed in his eyes to continue the leg work for him. He felt so close to the target now though. Pinning all the deaths on Littleton.

"Sir, a call for you," came the voice from the incident room.

"What is it?" asked Huws, having now got the bit between his teeth, piecing together his own timespan of known actions.

"They would like you to go to the farm in Allt Goch Sir, some very interesting finds apparently."

"Dammit," he uttered under his breath. He got up and grabbed his coat, patting the pocket to double check his car key was in it. "Give me the exact address then."

He grabbed the slip of paper and made for his car. He tapped the keypad to open the exit gate out of the compound and made his way east towards Allt Goch. Iesu Grist, he thought to himself, that village did not hold good memories for him. What, he wondered, would it throw at him now? Nothing, he desperately hoped to do with a big cat, though, as far as he knew cats didn't do drugs. He shook his head to himself, as he crossed the main road junction in the village of Pentraeth, the roads still relatively quiet with the threat of Covid still hanging over people, pleasant without the normal continuous stream of caravans, and boats and jet skis being towed by the static caravan owners of Benllech and beyond.

He found the farm entrance just off the main road, potholed to the point that a Dawn French comedic moment with the puddle would surely happen if it rained. He took his time, regretting bringing his own car and not taking one of the pool vehicles. Anyway, he was here now. He pulled up in the yard surprised to see the hunched figure of a man sitting in one of the squad cars.

"He kicked off when we arrived and said we were going to search the place. We had to detain and cuff him. We told him we had a warrant, but he was pretty agitated. We put the dog in the farmhouse but came up with nothing indoors apart from likely picking up some fleas." Reported one of the search team.

"Is he the father?" asked Huws.

"Yes Sir, William Huw Evans, though he claims to have very little to do with his son. His wife left him even before the boy was actually born it seems, they got divorced by the time the baby was two years old.

We have been going through the sheds one by one. Once the dog had dispersed the rats, he was allowed to search. The sheds are full of broken-down old farm machinery, some likely almost antique by now. But that shed over there is worth you looking at." He gestured with a nod of the head towards the rusting corrugated iron shed. Corners of the roof curled, and perforated, brown and red with rust, no doubt from winter thrashings by easterlies hurling themselves through poorly sheltered yard. Roofs leaking like colanders.

The door hinges rusting through the metal doorframes had been propped up by pointed rotting ends of old fence posts. A round hay feeder was propped against a second door, full to the brim of what looked like the black and green wrap off silage bales, along with tangled balled up nets and numerous plastic feed bags. Years old by the look of the slick green slime they were covered in. Huws stepped in to join the officers that were already emptying a large chest freezer of bagged up chunks of meat. Their prize was hidden underneath. Well packed and taped up bags of powder, an officer slit a bag and Huws just stopped himself from dipping his finger in the white powder and rubbing it under his upper lip- something he had done once in his career at the encouragement of his senior officer and had to be driven home high as a kite, much to the amusement of his Sergeant.

This was quite the haul, especially for this area. He wondered what Littleton had to say about that. Did he even know about this though? They piled the blocks into the back of the unmarked van. The SOCO officer took whatever prints he could get off the freezer and barn door and was told by Huws that as soon as he was done with prints that he was to put the old boy's meat supply back in the freezer.

Idris Huws strode up to the squad car and opened the door.

"Are you going to behave now if I uncuff you and let you out?"

The old boy glared at him and nodded, he held both hands out towards Huws. Freed, he got out of the car with a grunt and without a backward glance strode off towards the house.

"We need a word with you regarding your son," called Huws towards the retreating hunched back.

"I have no son, at least not one that gives me a second thought or consideration. Be sure to put my meat back in that freezer before it spoils, I've put a lot of effort into getting that."

Continuing towards the house away from Huws, he turned abruptly when Huws added that his son had met a tragic end, likely murder as it looked at the moment. His body would be released at some point soon when forensics were happy, they had all the evidence they needed, he could then be buried.

"Well, I certainly won't be paying for that, do you think I'm made of bloody money?"

He slammed the door behind him. Huws shook his head, feeling a degree of sympathy for the old boy struggling to make a living for himself out here. No doubt in the next couple of hours the reality of the loss of his son would hit him, but he had made it pretty clear there wasn't much love between them. The consequences of releasing the other bodies to God knows who struck him too, they hadn't as yet found a next of kin for the man known as Lee, that needed sorting pronto. What a sad reflection of broken up lives and family ties, they as police officers were often party to.

Getting back in his old car he carefully zig-zagged his way up the drive avoiding the sump smashing holes along the way, driving back to the office, wondering how the hell he was going to join all the dots now to put all of this in front of Littleton, but that is precisely what he was going to have to do, no doubt it would take a couple of them working through the night to piece together a foolproof interview for when they faced Littleton the next afternoon. His only decision so far had been not to take Justin Howard with him, it would be too hard for the lad and no doubt there would be arguments regarding his choice.

Chapter Forty

IDRIS HUWS WOKE up at 7 a.m. creased double having slept fitfully on the small couch in the rest room next to the kitchen at the station, not the best idea when he needed to be clear headed in a few hours' time. He hadn't put his weary head down until 2am, and still woke up with something he needed to write down on paper. He always kept a small bag of spare fresh clothes in his office, coffee cup in hand he walked through the incident room shocked to find a couple of his team already head down.

"Morning," he muttered as he passed their desk. "What are you up to at this early hour?"

"Sir, we are just typing up our notes from yesterday's search, nothing extra really that you don't know about, except that it has now been weighed. There was in all 130kg, which apparently would have a market value of around 15million. A very lucrative business it seems for young Evans. What we are unsure of is who he was working for, why was he storing the drugs as opposed to passing them on, is his old dad in on it and how do the other men enter into it. Were they bringing drugs in or were they taking it away? Was Evans selling them the drugs? Is there a whole local drug dealing industry that we are as yet not aware of? It's not quite the modus operandii of a county lines system that we are already aware of. Loads of questions, that hopefully if the interview is worded carefully, we can get it out of Littleton."

"Hmm," responded Huws. "This is potentially going to be the most difficult interview that I have had in my whole career. Rogers, would you like to come along with me to sit?"

The words had tumbled out of his mouth before he had really considered what he was asking of the young officer, but it was out there now.

"Oh gosh, yes please, yes Sir, I would be very happy to accompany you."

He continued to his office, grabbing the bag of clothes before disappearing into the sumptuous new shower rooms that the new station had installed. So much luxury in comparison to the old station, grant you, but a world away from the archaic historical building with its almost Dickensian atmosphere. He needed to stop moping about the good old days and move with the times.

By midday, both Huws and Rogers were on their way to the prison where Littleton was held awaiting trial, it was on the borders, almost a couple of hours drive away, but still their nearest prison and remand centre. Huws had taken a pool car, not wanting to add mileage to his own, it also afforded him the luxury of allowing Rogers to drive, giving him some headspace to organize his thoughts.

He shut his eyes once he had gone through the Conway tunnel, feigning sleep, Rogers talked a lot! It gave him a break. This was really not an interview that he anticipated would go necessarily as planned. In fact, he very much feared the worst, he had a very bad feeling about it.

They arrived at the security gate at one forty-five, just enough time to shake themselves free of the journey. They were both offered a cup of tea before they were to be taken to the interview room. It was explained to them that Littleton was at that moment in time talking to his brief, and by the sounds of it, the same woman that had been present at the first interview.

Huws took a deep breath when he was told that the room was

ready for him and tucked his file under his arm and led the way along the polished corridor floor to the door over which there was a light indicating it was in use.

They entered, Littleton looking much smaller than previously, slouched on his plastic chair. Grey tracksuit bottom and fleece top with velcroid pump type shoes on his feet. Prison issue. At least it looked as if he may have had a haircut and a shave.

Huws placed the file on the table in front of him, moving the adjacent chair out for Rogers to take a seat. He chose to remove his jacket, folding it carefully and slowly over the back of the chair on which he would shortly sit. Not once did he take his eyes off Littleton and not once did Littleton look at him.

Huws believed he recognized the look of a defeated man when he saw one. He felt slightly more confident. Brushing away some of the doubt that he felt on the journey.

Nodding across at Rogers she answered the unspoken question with a nod of her head. She was ready. Sitting down, he indicated that Rogers should push the electronic button to her side. Gone was the recording box that normally sat on the table, now the button was connected via Bluetooth to surround sound recorders. Nothing would be missed.

He started by introducing themselves, then asking Littleton to declare his name. The solicitor was staring him in the eyes, slightly giving him the heebie jeebies so intense was her stare. He did his best not to be drawn to look at her. He couldn't quite read the look; was it defeat or in fact confident triumph?

The conversation this time was a little different, none of the sullen arrogance that he had displayed previously. Huws had enough evidence in his armoury to put this man away for a very long time. What he needed to try to do was to piece together the rest of the crazy incidents. He hardly was able to absorb it all himself.

Barely had they started, Littleton in a hushed voice, almost inaudible, spoke. Huws asked him to speak up for the recording. He repeated.

"I will plead guilty to killing the policeman, I'm sorry I did that,

I felt at the time I had no other choice, I wish I had never done it, but I didn't kill the others, that wasn't me. If I plead guilty do you think I will get less of a sentence, it's more likely manslaughter isn't it?"

He looked alternatively from Huws to Rogers, with an occasional glance at his solicitor who up to now had not said a single word. She was far less sure of herself than at the initial interview. Huws didn't trust her one little bit. That statement however slightly took the wind out of his sails.

"That will be for the judge to decide," responded Huws gruffly. A vision of young Steffan gurgling his last, through a throatful of blood appeared in front of him. He momentarily closed his eyes before asking Littleton to go right back to where things had started down on the rocks above the beach that night where he was supposedly fishing with neither rod nor net. How could he explain what he was doing there?

Huws sat back in his chair, mirrored by young Rogers who was clearly waiting with baited-breath for the explanation if there was one forthcoming.

The story began, and as it developed it was slowly dawning on Huws that he may never be able to prove who did what in this situation. There were no live witnesses, unless one miraculously came out of the woodwork and he doubted that very much. He had a definite stomach churning feeling that Littleton and his brief were totally aware of this. Having no doubt spent the time between being caught and todays interview making up his story into a plausible 'woe is me tale', knowing full well, that other than the shooting of Parry nothing else could actually be pinned on him. He sat up a little in his seat, hands one atop the other on the table in front of him as if he was settling down to deliver a bedtime story woven from lies.

Chapter Forty-One

AND SO, it started. It was all Richard- Ricky Flints plan, he had stayed with him in his house in Essex when he had been kicked out, yet again by his wife.

Ricky's son was a no-good waste of space, but he knew a lad from Wales he had claimed who sailed yachts from place to place for owners. They had met him in a nightclub in Liverpool and when he'd had a few, he was bragging about how easy it was to make money on the side if you knew the right people. He took him home with him to his Liverpool flat for what turned out to be a drunken one- night stand where he divulged that he had contacts everywhere around the country and abroad, he was doing a fair trade from moving drugs around.

They never discovered where he actually lived but had heard through the grapevine that he wasn't always passing on all of the drugs he was carrying, a high-risk dangerous game but no one really took him to task about it because the amounts he kept back from each job was probably insignificant in the grand scheme of things and there was always the threat that he would expose the suppliers and dealers. He had left a phone number.

He was obviously supplying drugs to local dealers in his own time. Ricky was quite keen to get involved with this after his son had come to an arrangement with the lad and had invited him to come along for the ride which he had been happy to do.

Ricky's son and his mate were going to meet Ricky and himself on the coast. They had managed to get a boat, apparently, one of those big rubber dinghy things.

Both he and Ricky were going to meet this lad on the clifftop somewhere on Anglesey where it was supposed to be quiet and a bit off the beaten track. Ricky had got hold of some cash somewhere, a significant amount, to pay for the drugs. He never divulged where it came from. He reckoned that we would make a killing on it back down south.

He said his son and his mate would meet us there with the boat, once Ricky had handed over the money, his son would take the bags in the boat back towards Liverpool where Ricky had organized to meet them so there was no chance of being caught out with any gear on them.

He continued with his fairy tale, becoming more akin to a Brother's Grim tale by the minute. He didn't know why the hell Ricky wanted his useless son involved, but he supposed he was the contact point for the yacht bloke.

"So, you have no idea what the yacht bloke as you call him was called?" butted in Rogers.

Huws cleared his throat, slightly taken aback by Rogers breaking into the flow of conversation. He ignored her and raised his eyebrows at Littleton, awaiting his response, acknowledging that it was perfectly fine for him to answer her question. It had just been unexpected that's all. Littleton did not even grace her with a look, just answered looking directly at Huws.

He answered in the negative. He had no idea what he was called. There was no need for him to know according to Ricky.

The meeting had been arranged for a time when the tide would be at the right height for the boat to come alongside the rocks, the lads had been making headway along the coast during the day and had hung about near the island nearby. The supplier would meet them at the agreed spot, the exchange would be made, the lads in the boat would make off with the drugs and he and Ricky would make their way from the area overnight in the car to meet the boys at a prearranged location.

"What made you think you could trust Flint junior not to disappear with the haul, never to be seen again?" asked Huws.

"Because he was shit scared of his father, they didn't really get on, but he knew which side his bread was buttered and knew he would get a quarter share at least in what we picked up. He was a junkie and was desperate to do anything to secure his next hit."

He paused at this point, seeming to almost forget the drift of where the story was taking him. A sure sign thought Huws that a lot of what they were hearing was likely fabricated.

With the other witnesses to the truth all dead, Littleton knew he had them over a barrel and could likely say what he wanted.

Taking a deep breath, "Go on," encouraged Huws, anticipating exactly where this tale of woe was leading. Despondency already creeping in on him.

Littleton continued.

The boat had arrived and tucked into the rocks biding their time. 'Yacht man,' as they called him turned up late, by which time Ricky was getting more and more agitated.

He seemed to be worried about trusting the guy to handover the drugs, going on about getting the drugs in his hands first before handing over the cash, agitated, as he had told the guy to bring the haul in a rucksack and telling Littleton that he would need to check it before he handed over the cash, as far as he knew the bloke might have packaged up some sugar or flour. He needed to be sure and he needed Littleton to intervene if there was any risk of some sort of trickery. He admitted that he would have been ok with delivering a beating if he had to, having given and taken a fair few beatings in his lifetime. He smiled at Huws at this point.

"Go on man, what the hell are you expecting a medal?" Huws fought back his anger. Rogers looked across at him fearing her boss may just lose it. However, it appeared that he rapidly composed himself. "Get on with it, what happened next?"

Littleton continued his likely fabrication. Yacht man had

arrived, he was on foot, having clearly walked in from somewhere, he hadn't come down the lane but approached along the clifftop, maybe he lived locally or had left a car nearby. He'd probably been watching and sussing things out from a distance. Anyway, he clambered down to where they were, appearing quite arrogant, just in his stance, not a word did he speak, he just held his hand out towards Ricky, indicating he wanted the cash.

Ricky had laughed at him and told him to hand over the rucksack first, that he wasn't getting a penny until he had checked the bag. The lad seemed quite biddable and confident and immediately handed over the bag. Ricky turned his back and opened the bag, then all of a sudden, he had pulled a revolver out of the bag that the cash was in and shot the lad, and literally kicked him over the edge into the sea. It had happened so quickly they were all surprised. He had totally lost it; Littleton claimed he realised his mate had a plan which at best didn't involve the rest of them. Greed you see, total greed.

"Go on," encouraged Huws. "We found the lads body shortly after the other two, seemed he managed to get himself cut up by a propellor too."

Littleton seemed mildly shaken by this, probably not the death, just the horror of the consequences.

Rogers was busy taking notes, the solicitor, head down, could not even meet his eyes. She appeared to be picking a thread from the edge of her shirt cuff.

Littleton cleared his throat. The next few minutes had caught him out, he claimed. It had happened so quickly; Ricky's son was at the helm of the boat and he would imagine now, with hindsight that killing the supplier was always in their plan. They fired up the engine and came around below us, I expected Ricky to throw them the bag, instead he shot the lad who was at the back of the boat, waiting to catch the bag and before you know it he had shot his own son. He repeated this feigning shock at the sheer awfulness of the outcome.

At this point the boat was adrift, moving slightly away from us. Littleton claimed he couldn't tell if the men were dead at this point, but he knew they were in a bad way just by how quickly the bottom of the boat was swilling with blood.

He guessed things were not looking good for him now either. Flint had turned towards him, with a look on his face that he never wanted to see again, the look of a madman, quick as a flash he realised the need to defend himself. He barreled himself towards him fully expecting gunfire, knocking him off balance and thankfully managed to knock the gun out of his hand. Ricky had lost it completely; Littleton claimed he was fighting for his life.

He paused at this point in his delivery, almost as if he was expecting a display of sympathy from the two officers sitting ahead of him, non-came.

At some point in those few minutes, Ricky fell backwards in the desperate skirmish, Littleton managing to sit astride him holding his arms down but he had obviously had a bang on the back of his head, he wasn't responding. Littleton claimed that he didn't know what to do, it was self defence. He looked dead; he wasn't sure he was dead but in the spur of the moment he had pushed him over the ledge into the sea.

He regretted not trying to help him.

Huws just shook his head at this point knowing full well that he would have had no intention of helping him.

He needed to get away, grabbed the bags and the gun, and put everything in one bag, but in making to climb back up the hill he realised that his leg was hurting, probably twisted in the fight.

He had called 999 to get someone to help him, he told them he had been fishing and fallen. It was dark by then and Ricky being over the edge could not be seen and the boat was drifting away on the tide. The Coastguard arrived and an ambulance but eventually he persuaded them all that he was fine to make his way own way. He described how he had even pretended to have been a little inebriated and fallen.

He claimed to have left the car there, but hid until they had gone, going back for the car then driving around the back lanes for a while. He came to a dead end but found the cottage along the lane, which on checking over was empty.

He and Ricky had purchased a few bits of food to eat later at the local shop so he decided to hide out until any dust that might arise could settle. He announced that from that point on they knew the rest.

With a hint of a smirk that Huws wanted to smack off his face, he repeated his admission of guilt in his part in the shooting of the young officer. He never meant to kill him, he whined pathetically, in fact he had never shot a gun before, but had nothing to do with the others and that greedy bastard Ricky banged his head when he fell.

"There is nothing else you can pin on me."

Huws looked at him with utter contempt, knowing full well that time would only have allowed him to set his story in stone, there was virtually nothing in their armoury that would disprove it. Huws immediately copied by Rogers collected his folder up and left the room- seething. He could not possibly be angrier. That went for the bloody solicitor too.

It was quite a silent journey home. Both he and the young Rachel Rogers clearly deep in their own thoughts and despair at their realization that their man might well get away with the murder of at least four people.

Chapter Forty-Two

LITTLETON HAD BEEN ESCORTED BACK to his cell, beaming from ear to ear as the cell door closed behind him. He could barely control his mirth as the officers had walked heavy footed away along the corridor. He burst into manic laughter; he couldn't believe that the cops had swallowed his story. He sat on the hard, wooden bed and almost rolled about like an overgrown child chuffed at getting an unexpected prize.

The difference was, this was expected, things had worked out almost to plan, ok, he admitted to himself that he had not planned on his hideout being busted or the bloody copper standing right in his way.

He had plotted his plan for weeks after Ricky had discussed it with him, in fact, he had even taken a train up to Bangor and sussed out the territory as soon as he knew the exchange location.

The gun had been given to him by an old acquaintance who owed him a favour.

Shooting yacht man had been a doddle, shooting the lads had not been quite so easy, Ricky had gone for him when he had grabbed the bag and insisted that Ricky hand him the money. Ricky managed to get a punch in to his face but nothing that stopped him in his tracks, he was used to worse.

At that point his son had started to clamber ashore, to help his dad so he got what he deserved and fell back into the inflatable. Ricky at that point had turned back so quickly to check his son that he had simply slipped and cracked his head open, served him right the greedy bastard, he had treated him like a skivvy for years, getting him to do his dirty work for him. Always the one to take the flack. It had even cost him his marriage, so that was his own bloody fault, the other lad at this point had leapt to the helm and was clearly going to make off.

He couldn't risk him getting away and dobbing him in so despite not being an accomplished shot he knew he had hit him as he was speeding away. He had heard him shout out in pain. He had been glad it was dark as he watched the boat drift off on the tide.

His job was done. He pushed both Yacht man and Ricky over the edge. Unfortunately, Ricky got snagged on a jagged rock, and sort of hung horizontally just above the water. No matter the tide might just lift him off the sharp rock and take him away to God knows where in the same direction as yacht man.

He knew he would do a fair bit of time, a fair few years , maybe a bit less if he kept his nose clean, but hopefully if he was not too decrepit and old, and more importantly still in ownership of all his marbles, he might still enjoy the fruits of his labour when he returned to his escape route of that day, to pick up the bags that he had taken out of the rucksack for his own enjoyment, holed up in the cottage.

One bag he had left in the car, with multiple small packages in, the police had found that, but there were four packages in all to split between them. The police had that one, he had hidden the other three in the depths of one of the quarry tunnels where he had hidden that night. Digging the hole had been quite easy even with his bare hands, once he broke through the top crust of air- dried cow dung, underneath was a fine albeit rank smelling powder. The big rock he had placed on top would hopefully keep them hidden and prevent the cows from crapping on them. Praying the haul would not decompose with age, he was quite chuffed with his inventiveness. Barely could he stop grinning.

Knowing it would be a long time before he could retrieve his bounty there would be enough money from the selling of it to see him through his old age, he could only hope for the best and a lot of good luck. His brief had virtually guaranteed him she could get the charge reduced to manslaughter if luck was on their side.

His court date was soon, he felt supremely confident that there was no way they could pin the rest on him.

He slept well that night, he just needed to go over and over his carefully spun fairy tale lest he be interviewed again. He needed to ingrain the story deep into his brain. He would repeat it to himself daily until he knew it off by heart- after all he had nothing else pressing to do. Prison didn't really scare him. A room, food, telly, drugs- if you got to know the right people. Better by far than being on Ricky's settee in all his filth.

Chapter Forty-Three

IT WAS a solemn DI Huws who walked into the incident room the following day. Rogers was already in her seat and clearly by the atmosphere had already filled the team in on the interview result.

Huws laid his jacket on the back of his old office chair, cleared his throat and went through to talk to the awaiting crew. They looked at him with expectation and disappointment in equal measure. Knowing full well that Huws was going to tell them that Littleton had at least admitted to shooting their friend and colleague Steffan but was most certainly not admitting to any of the other murders despite Huws knowing full well that he had just spun them a well-practiced cock and bull story.

They had nothing on him, just five dead men and absolutely nothing tangible to prove Littleton killed the other four.

It was a disaster on their patch really.

A big job, a lot of man hours for which again DI Huws would no doubt take the brunt from the DCI, just like the other cases a couple of years before that some of the team here had been involved with, but that was how the dice had rolled. There was nothing currently, unless someone waved a magic wand and found some solid evidence, that they could use to get him.

PC Howard was visibly saddened by the result, pleased that Steff would get his justice but sad that a clearly evil human being would likely get away with multiple murders.

"The only way in the short term with this," added Huws to his delivery, "is that until the trial which is only a week away, we interview him again, and maybe present him with some other piece of evidence that may, if we're lucky, cause him to maybe repeat his story but if we aim to confuse him with what we know at this side, maybe, he will tangle himself up and we can catch him out.

We have a lot of work ahead of us now and it needs to be done in a very short window of time, we need to look into the minutiae of everything we already know."

Huws looked around the room, the team's brains were clearly engaging as a few made notes on paper, others scrolled and tapped at computer keyboards. They were a good gang, albeit young and only just exploring their detective talents, this case had been a real baptism of fire for a few of them.

He was proud of them. Time would tell on this case; he knew they couldn't throw more and more of the British taxpayer's money at this, and it may well be a case that would find its conclusion after he had retired from the force.

His gut feeling told him that the man had guilt running through every cell of his body. He knew he would go down for Parry's murder, but finding he was responsible for the others would make sure he never saw the light of day again. He tasked the team to deal with next of kin contacting, for the victims still lying in the mortuary, their bodies were virtually ready for release, any family members that could be found needed to be contacted. He wasn't actually sure if anyone would claim them. That task may well also fall to the state.

He thanked the team, encouraging them to continue following every possible avenue for that week at least and despondently turned away and entered his own glass walled office.

Huws sat kneading his hands together in a subconscious display of weariness.

His phone pinged, a text had arrived, he did not recognize the number as one he had stored in his address book, he was pretty useless like that. The message cheered him up more than he had expected on reading it.

Jane, wanting to meet, if he had time over the weekend only if he was able to spare a few hours if he wasn't too busy. She offered to prepare a picnic again and maybe they could choose a nice area of the Anglesey Coastal path for a walk or the Llyn peninsula.

He realised that this made his face crack into a smile, something that had become an alien feeling for him this last year and more. It felt good. He answered her text, suggesting the Llyn. She responded immediately, she would take him to Tydweiliog, they would start the walk with a coffee at a lovely farm-based café and shop called Cwt Tatws that she loved visiting, from there they would venture along the coast following the Coastal path to the left, and have their picnic at Porth y Cychod, which was a glorious little bay which still had the old fishermen's huts on the cliffside down to the shore. Even on a blustery day, they could find some shelter in the lee of one of the huts. No doubt they would see a fair few seals too, she added that she always did. She insisted that they take the dogs for the day too.

He knew this walk well from having been with Gwen, he was a little hesitant but maybe just maybe it might go a little way towards putting a few memories to rest awhile and create some new ones.

He didn't mention this fact to Jane. He didn't want to spoil it for her.

Huws left work that day feeling different somehow. They had got their man for Steffan Parry's murder and he had a childlike excitement at a possible new friendship if not more, peeping over the horizon. He wouldn't count his chicken quite yet on that score, however.

All he wished for on top of this now was for the Covid Pandemic and all its lockdowns and deaths and endless regulations to disappear.

Chapter Forty-Four

WILLIAM HUW EVANS grunted with effort as he arose from his threadbare armchair, old stinking flattened cushions placed on the seat to soften the pressure from the slowly erupting springs which just added to his discomfort.

He slept in the chair now, not venturing up the stairs to his bed, his painful hips preventing the nightly climb.

Boots on his feet day and night, the inability to bend his joints to remove them causing too much pain. In fact, he couldn't really remember when he had changed any of his clothes last. No matter, no one visited particularly since this pandemic thing started, it made no real difference to him other than when he visited the local town for his basics when he wrapped an old scarf around his face, having been harshly told off by some woman for not having a mask. Hmph, he thought grumpily, strange days.

Tonight, he would be having a bit of a treat, after the police had been and taken all the packets out of his freezer that his son put there, he was once again able to reach the meat he had stored in the bottom.

His son had warned him on the threat of death not to touch anything. He had begrudgingly agreed to him feeding the generator with fuel on a regular basis to keep the freezer running. He darent cross him, he knew the sort of company he kept.

That afternoon, he had walked the hedgerows picking up old dry branches that had broken off the boundary vegetation, during the years high winds, some he wisely ignored, so covered were they with black fungal growth, but he had enough to keep a fire going for a few hours and cook a nice rolled and boned upper section of thigh that he had managed to retrieve from the depths of the freezer.

It would be a tasty meal tonight with a hunk of the loaf he had purchased in the town bakery and would certainly be tasty served cold over the next few days. His hungry old tummy gnawed at him in anticipation. He never really considered anymore what he was actually eating. He was no longer morally disturbed at the actual source of his meat supply.

Likely he would never manage to achieve such a kill again due to his lessening strength, but that big old wildcat, whatever it was, had done him a huge favour a couple of years ago and no one had been any the wiser. He could barely believe that the police officers who handled all the meat had not even given it a second thought, as far as they were concerned it was probably beef and lamb. This actually made him laugh, a deep belly laugh that erupted out of his depths, a rarity. He had by now absorbed the news that his son seemed to have been murdered. Likely by the big drug runners he seemed to have become entangled with, but in all honesty other than the blood tie, he meant very little to him. He had continued his mothers venomous dislike of his father and had not a single care towards him at all.

Someone else could bear the brunt of burying him.

Ha! Maybe he should just add him to the freezer supply. He guffawed again, tickled by his own ideas.

Later that evening a very satiated Evans sat back in his chair and snoozed in the fading glow and heat of his fire embers, stains of fat juice running down the front of his old check shirt. A young nervous rat silently manouvering around his feet picking up remnants of bread crumbs and partially chewed gristle that Evans had spat out as being too tough to chew.

Evans kicked it away when it crept onto his boots to lick a drop of melted fat. It scuttled away, no doubt to crawl up into the bottom of the chewed-out chair on which he was sitting, joining the two-day old littler of blind, bald babies that she had just had.

No doubt in the not-too-distant future thought Evans, likely he himself would become a satisfying meal for a family of rats.

About the Author

The author lives on the island of Anglesey on the Northern tip of North Wales, her interests are firmly in the outdoors, walking the coasts and the hills. A retired college lecturer and a Coach and Examiner for the British Horse Society. She now trains people in first Aid.

Her main love was horse breeding alongside her late husband and business partner. Also active as a voluntary Coastguard officer for the last 23 years she spends her time waiting for a pager call and dreaming of writing that successful novel in her spare time. She also plays in a brass band.

She has, as with her previous published works, drawn on her life experience to write this book. Her previous books being equestrian topics, an older children's book 'On the run' and the first in this DI Huws series called 'Community killing.

Also by Anne Roberts

DI Huws Book 1 Community Killing

DI Huws Book 3 Community Confessions

On the Run- a stand alone short story

Printed by Amazon Italia Logistica S.r.l.
Torrazza Piemonte (TO), Italy

42288961R00103